INJURED HEROES SERIES - BOOK FOUR

CROSSROADS OF
OBSESSION

DANIELLE M HAAS

To Celeste. My sounding board, my cheerleader, and one of the strongest women I know. Thank you for your unending support and being a living example of where hard work and a kind heart can take you. You deserve the very best in this world.

1

Elizabeth Gilmore kept her mouth shut and a fake smile plastered on her face as she stared across her desk at Paul Stevens, the chair of the Arts and Science department. Only the chance to earn tenure kept her from throttling the man asking her yet again to grab dinner.

"Come on, Lizzie. It's just a meal. We can talk about how I can help you advance your career a little faster." He grinned, and the corners at his gray eyes crinkled.

She fought not to wince at the nickname. Only one person ever called her Lizzie, and he was the one man she never wanted to see again.

Casting a quick glance at the clock mounted in the back of her office, she frowned. "I have plans tonight. Besides, there might not be any written rules regarding staff spending time together off campus, but I think it's frowned upon."

She actually had no idea what the rulebook said about dating a colleague, but she'd throw whatever excuse she could at him. Even if it were allowed, she'd never fall for his fake charm and arrogance. Not after struggling to get over losing the man who'd finally broken through her defenses then left her a grieving mess.

What she'd like to do is use all her training and kick the snot out of the pompous ass who refused to take no for an answer, but he had too much sway with the dean. One wrong move could cost her a lot.

A soft knock on the door disrupted her thoughts, and Sebastian Tillman, fellow professor and friend, popped his head in the room. "Staff meeting in ten minutes."

She offered him a genuine smile, grateful for the interruption. Tidying her desk, she rose. "Thanks for the reminder. Don't want to be late."

Paul rolled his eyes. "If you're with me, you're never late."

She fought the urge to gag.

Sebastian raised his dark eyebrows in an exaggerated show of amusement and waved before heading back into the hall.

"Shall we go?" She asked, not wanting to be trapped in this room with Paul a second longer. Besides, after the meeting she'd be free to go and get her daughter—her summer open with no classes to teach and months of fun activities ahead. Today, she planned to take her on a new hiking trail through the mountains, one she'd just discovered that hugged a gentle stream where Audrey could dip her feet in and splash around.

The image pulled at her heart strings. Her four-year-old daughter was her entire world. The reason she quit her job as a profiler with the FBI and chose a safer path as a college professor. Audrey had already lost one parent. She couldn't lose another.

A slight curve twisted Paul's lips. "Maybe we should discuss a plan to help get you that tenured position before we go to the meeting. I have a few ideas that could really boost your appeal to the dean."

Disgust squeezed her insides. Over the past year, he'd made it perfectly clear what she'd need to do in order to secure his help. "I appreciate the offer, but I'm confident I'll either get the promotion of my own merit, or it will go to someone more deserving."

Paul fell back into his seat and swatted his hand in the air as if shoving aside an annoying gnat. "Don't be silly."

Pushing a coil of blond hair behind her ear, she pieced together the right words in her brain before she said something she'd regret. "It really is nice of you to offer, but—"

A shrill siren screamed through the air and water sprayed down from the ceiling. Panic surged through Elizabeth, and she glanced around the room as if she'd find the reason for the blaring close by.

"What the hell?" Paul yelled against the screeching fire alarm. "We need to get out of here."

Paul circled an arm around the small of her back and led her to the door. Shivers danced along her spine, though she wasn't sure if it was from the ice-cold water raining down on her or the way Paul's wide palm molded against her hip.

"If there's a fire, maybe we should make sure everyone gets outside." She stepped away from his touch and yelled over her shoulder as scurrying faculty members hurried past.

Paul ignored her comments and pushed her forward.

Her gaze darted around the chaos, searching for flames. The exit sign loomed ahead, and her heart fluttered. An image of her four-year-old daughter flashed in her mind, and she quickened her pace. If something happened to her, Audrey wouldn't have anyone.

"Almost there," Paul said, urging her onward.

She pushed against the thick metal bar of the door and sunlight flooded her sight. She squinted against the blinding glare of the May sun while welcoming the rays of warmth against her goose pimpled flesh. Water dripped from her clothes as she crossed a grassy patch of lawn and stepped onto the concrete pavilion, joining the shivering crowd. She scanned the area for familiar faces, but Paul gripped her bicep and pulled her aside.

She yanked out of his grasp. "Stop," she said between clenched teeth. "I don't need you pulling me around." Emergency sirens echoed through the valley of Elm Ridge, Tennessee, startling birds as they squawked overhead. "I need to find out what happened. I need to help."

"What the hell can you do?" Condescension dripped from his words. "Let's get out of here. We can talk more about your promotion."

She turned to face him; she'd finally had enough of his bullshit.

Bang!

Terror paralyzed her at the sound of a gunshot. Memories of another gunshot ripped into her, making her feel the pain of losing the man she loved all over again—stealing her ability to separate the past from the present.

Paul stumbled back and the iron fist of fear gripped her heart. Shouts of panic rose around her, and people dropped to the ground. Elizabeth fell to her stomach and covered the back of her head with trembling hands. She squeezed her eyes shut as adrenaline coursed through her veins. Her flight or fight instinct kicked in and the urge to jump up and run like hell made her limbs quiver. But who knew what she'd be running into—or if she'd be making herself a better target for whoever had just shot into the crowd?

Please God, don't let there be another gun shot. Please don't let me die.

Her heart hammered against the hard ground beneath her. Did the fire alarm go off to force them to leave the security of the building, making them all sitting ducks for the psychopath with a gun? Whatever had happened, they all needed to get out of there.

She raised her head from the ground and scanned the

shell-shocked members of the crowd climbing to their feet. Screaming sirens and muffled sobs rang in her ears. No more shots echoed against the sky. No stomping feet or angry demands clued her into someone planning to cause more destruction. Now was the time to run for cover.

Something warm and sticky brushed against her hand and her stomach rolled. On a deep breath, Elizabeth turned toward Paul. Wolf-like eyes stared back at her, but no life lingered behind his pupils. Thick, crimson blood oozed from his chest and splattered the ground around her, spanning the distance between them. She gasped for air, but her throat tightened, making it hard to breathe. The world spun and slowly the blue skies melted into darkness.

THE SUN BEAT down on Tucker Clayman as he threw another large bag of dog food into the back of his truck. He wiped sweat from his forehead with the back of his arm, grateful to be done with his list of errands for the day. Leaving Pine Valley always set him on edge, even when only traveling to the next town over.

But it couldn't be helped. Not when he was responsible for a whole kennel of therapy dogs back at Crossroads Mountain Retreat. Living in a small town nestled in the Smoky Mountains might be ideal for a former officer with a host of emotional baggage, but the lack of supplies in the mom-and-pop stores could be a pain in the ass. Especially when the supplies he needed could be found in the town where Lizzie lived.

A familiar ache in his chest had him rubbing the heel of his hand over his heart. He wished stopping in Elm Ridge meant he could swing by her place for a quick hello. Maybe tell Audrey stories about the father she'd never know.

The father who'd been killed all because of one stupid decision on Tucker's part.

But that fantasy would never come true. Lizzie hated him, as she should, and as much as he hated to admit it, he knew it wasn't guilt that kept him from trying to soften her toward him. The feelings he'd stuffed deep down since the moment he laid eyes on her—the same moment Gary had seen her and claimed he'd fallen head over heels—prevented him from attempting to right his wrongs.

Resolving to stop dwelling on the past, Tucker unlocked the truck and hopped inside. A blast of cold air slammed against him, and his black lab mix leaned over the center console and licked the side of his face.

"Really, Otto?" He laughed and wiped off the slobber. "Ready to head home?"

Otto gave one bark and settled back in his seat.

Tucker ruffled the top of Otto's soft head then secured his seatbelt. Being close to his best buddy always calmed his nerves. Luckily there weren't many places he couldn't bring Otto along in the small town he'd grown up in. It helped that he worked at a retreat dedicated to aiding injured law enforcement and veterans. His job also allowed him to use the skills he'd picked up at the K-9 unit to show others how the love and patience of a dog can be transformative.

The blaring siren of a fire engine pitched anxiety high in his chest. A flash of red blazed by, followed by another and bookended by an ambulance. That couldn't be good.

Alarm had him grabbing his phone and calling his buddy Cruz, a police officer in Pine Valley.

"Hey, Tucker. I can't really talk right now," Cruz said. "I'm on my way to Elm Ridge. The local station there has called in for back up."

Two police cars flew by, red and blue lights slashing against the beautiful afternoon sky. Tucker might not know what the emergency was, but if there was a chance he could help, he had to act. "What's going on?" he asked as he pulled onto the street and followed the speeding cruisers.

"Shooter at the college."

The words fisted his stomach. Lizzie worked at the college, but that didn't mean she was in trouble. Hell, classes had been done for a few days. Chances were slim she was even at the campus, let alone in the exact spot where a shooter was present. "I'm in Elm Ridge. I'll head toward the college, just in case they need an extra set of hands."

He might not be an officer anymore, but he was trained and more than capable to assist in an emergency. Even if the thought of jumping into the action made his palms sweat and heart pound against his chest like an anvil.

"You sure you're up for that?"

No, but he couldn't say that. Couldn't admit that even after all this time, fear kept him on the sidelines. "I'll be fine. Besides, Elm Ridge is just as small as Pine Valley. They're not equipped to deal with something like this."

"True. I'll call when I get there. I'm about ten minutes out."

Tucker disconnected and tightened his grip on the steering wheel. Otto sat straight, gaze fixed out the window and hair on the nape of his neck standing tall. The animal always sensed Tucker's moods, and he didn't doubt his canine companion would jump into the fray if needed. That's what he'd been trained to do, even if an injury kept him from fulfilling the duties for which he'd been bred.

The quaint downtown streets and line of businesses disappeared, replaced by patches of thick forest and a winding road. Tucker kept close to the police officers in front of him, making the turn down the lane that led to the campus. Young saplings lined the road and a sign that read Elm Ridge Community College announced he'd arrived.

A mess of emergency vehicles and frantic pedestrians filled

the lot. He weaved between them, finding a spot to park. "Sorry, boy. You'll need to stay here. I'll keep the air on for you, and I'll try not to be long."

Otto whined in protest, but Tucker couldn't chance bringing him into danger.

He shut the door and muscled his way through the crowd as he approached the man-made barrier at the edge of the property. He darted his gaze in every direction. His heartrate kicked up as he took in the scene—the firefighters blasting a torrent of water onto the far side of the building, swirls of black smoke spiraling toward white clouds, a rushing swarm of police officers scouring the area.

Tucker dipped under the crime scene tape and jogged to the closest policewoman.

The officer spun toward him with her hand on the butt of her gun. "You can't be back here."

Tucker stopped on the corner of the pavilion and held his palms in the air in front of him. "My name's Tucker Clayman, former officer. I just want to offer my assistance."

The young woman stared at him with a grim set of her mouth. "I appreciate that. Still doesn't mean I can let you onto the crime scene."

He glanced down and a puddle of blood made him hesitate. Sweat beaded at his temple and he swallowed hard before returning his gaze to the cherub-faced officer with wide eyes. "I understand. I'll get out of your way but stay close by in case I'm needed." The last thing he wanted was to step on anyone's toes, but he couldn't leave. Not yet.

"Tucker!"

The panicked sound of his name had him turning toward the street. He'd know that voice anywhere.

Lizzie.

A line of ambulances cluttered the sidewalk. He ran toward them, and his pulse pounded as fast as his sprinting legs. The back doors of one ambulance were open wide, and Lizzie sat on a gurney inside. Raw, cold fear rushed through him and erased all the reasons he needed to stay away from Elizabeth Gilmore. He launched himself into the ambulance and secured her safely in his arms.

She fisted his shirt in her hands and her entire body trembled against him.

He pulled away to see her face. Tears ran down her dirt-smeared cheeks, the moisture making her deep hazel eyes sparkle. He cupped her jaw in his hand and brushed a tear away with the pad of his thumb. "Are you okay? Are you hurt?" He tried to stop the quiver in his voice, but damn, he'd never known what terror was until this moment.

His finger brushed against something sticky on her jawline, and he leaned back to take a closer look. A spot of blood stained her face and the top half of her once-white shirt. Anger smashed against him like a tidal wave, and he clenched his jaw to keep his temper in check. Someone had hurt her, and when he found out who it was, he'd kill the sonofabitch.

2

The heat of Tucker's touch burned Elizabeth's cheek, but she couldn't break away. At least not yet. Not when terror still swirled inside her like a hurricane. She stared into the depths of his cobalt blue eyes to anchor herself. Her breath evened out and the frantic beat of her heart slowed to a normal rhythm.

Then reality slammed against her.

She reared back and wiped at her face. "I'm fine. The blood isn't mine." Her voice caught on the last word, an image of Paul's dead eyes making bile slosh in her stomach.

As if aware of the turmoil his touch caused, Tucker shoved his hands in the front pockets of his jeans. "Good. I mean...I'm sorry someone else was shot, but I'm glad it wasn't you."

She nodded, understanding what he meant.

A beat of awkward silence passed. Chaos reigned outside the little bubble of the ambulance. She licked her dry lips, wishing she could put into words the million questions racing around her mind. But right now, only one of them mattered. "What are you doing here?"

He dropped his gaze and rubbed the back of his neck. "I

was in town running errands. Called a buddy of mine who told me what had happened, so I just showed up. In case they needed an experienced officer with medical training. I didn't think, I just came."

His confession would have coerced a smile if her stomach wasn't rebelling against the panic continuing to erupt outside. Jumping into the thick of things was at the core of who he was and was also the reason the father of her child was no longer here.

The thought sobered her, and she scooted farther away from him and crossed her arms over her chest. Her wet t-shirt clung to her skin, and the late-spring heat made the blanket wrapped around her shoulders unbearable.

A middle-aged emergency responder approached them. Dampness stained the blue of his shirt and a dazed look she'd often seen in the field dominated his face. "How you doing?"

She straightened on the gurney. Being seen as a victim or a patient weren't things she relished. Life had thrown her a lion's share of troubles, and she didn't want to be seen as weak by anyone. Especially not Tucker. "Fine. I'd like to leave."

"Your vitals are good, and there's no medical reason to keep you any longer. If you've given your statement to the police, you're welcome to go. If you have any other symptoms, or pass out again, call for help immediately."

"You passed out?" Tucker balled his hands into fists at his side. "Are you sure you're okay to drive?"

"As I already said, I'm fine." She kept her tone calm as if telling Audrey to pick up her shoes for the fifth time and she didn't want to yell. "All I want is to get home and see my daughter."

A vein ticked above his eyebrow, and he jumped out of the ambulance. He backed up to allow her space to exit, then extended a hand.

She hesitated, then slipped her palm in his as she stepped

outside. The warmth of his skin made her pulse jump. She quickly pulled her hand back and wiped it on the side of her dress pants, hoping to erase any lingering feelings of excitement from his touch. "Thank you for checking on me, but I'm all right. I'll see you soon."

She turned to walk away then stopped, slumping her shoulders forward.

"What is it?" he asked, staying planted on the manicured grass.

His velvety voice skimmed the back of her neck, and dread slowed her movements as she spun back around with a frown. "I don't have my things. My purse, keys, phone...everything is inside the building."

The EMT locked the back of the ambulance. "I don't think they're letting anyone back in the building yet. The firefighters are still working on the fire."

She let her head drop forward. Her arms ached to hold her daughter, and not only was she stuck on the campus with no way to get home, but she couldn't even get ahold of her nanny to let Courtney know she was okay.

Tucker cleared his throat. "I can take you. If you want."

She closed her eyes against the crushing blow of her situation. All she wanted was for Tucker to leave her alone, but her desire to see her daughter outweighed everything else. "Thank you."

He dipped his chin then led her through the parking lot. Her water-logged shoes slapped onto the asphalt and the brilliant rays of sun streamed down on her. She lifted her chin and welcomed the penetrating warmth. She fought the urge to glance behind her. She didn't want to see the place she loved flooded with cops and stained in blood.

Elizabeth furrowed her brow and took in the faces of curious pedestrians clogging the parking lot. What were they doing? A horrible, violent crime had just occurred, and the shooter was at large. Weren't they scared? Didn't they want to be hidden away so they weren't the next victims to fall to the ground when a shot rang out from nowhere?

A prickle of apprehension tickled the back of her neck as if someone watched her. She darted her gaze up and down the sidewalks, but nothing stood out. Logic told her whoever had killed Paul Stevens wouldn't be hiding among small houses or the smattering of trees that lined the perimeter of the school, but logic couldn't beat back terror. Fear churned inside her, and she craved the safety of Tucker's vehicle. She quickened her stride until she reached the old truck.

A large, black dog sat in the passenger seat and her stomach dropped. "Is that..." She couldn't bring herself to say the dog's name, even though it was etched in her memory.

Tucker nodded then skirted around her and opened the door. "Otto, in the back."

The dog leapt over the seat and settled onto the bench in the second row.

She cast the canine a quick glance, nerves tightening her stomach, then climbed in and fastened her seatbelt. Otto's heavy pants made it impossible to pretend he wasn't there, but she refused to acknowledge him. Cold air blasted from the vents. She fiddled with her seatbelt and clasped her hands in her lap while waiting for Tucker to hurry the hell up and get in the vehicle. The driver's side door opened, and relaxed her muscles.

"Here." Tucker handed her his phone, turned on the engine, and drove away from the campus. "Call anyone you'd like."

"Thanks." Elizabeth punched in the familiar number of her nanny and pressed the device to her ear. The outline of the Smoky Mountains rose above the horizon, and all she wanted was to run. Escape. Grab her daughter and build a brand-new life far away from the nightmare she'd just survived.

She'd done it once. She could do it again.

The phone barely completed its connection when Courtney's panicked voice crashed into Elizabeth's ear. "Hello? Who's this?"

"Courtney. It's me. Elizabeth."

"Oh my God, are you all right? I'm watching the news right now. There was a shooter at the college?"

Shock leaked from her system, replaced by fatigue and a primal urge to hug her daughter. But that would have to wait. "I need you to get Audrey out of the house for a little bit."

"Why? Are you hurt? What happened?"

Elizabeth sighed and fought to keep the strain from her voice. "I'm okay, but my clothes are a mess. My shirt's covered in blood. I don't want Audrey to see that. I'll tell you the rest later."

"Okay. Audrey and I can go back to the park. You take all the time you need. Just let me know when to bring her home."

"You can't take her anywhere in town. It's not safe. The shooter's at large." Elizabeth choked out the word, and Tucker hovered his hand over hers as if he wanted to grab hold of her again before returning it to the steering wheel. She hated to admit it, but if he wasn't here, she'd have crumbled into a million pieces.

"Have her sitter take her to the park in Pine Valley," Tucker said, voice tight and eyes fixed straight ahead. "She'll be safe there. I can drive you when you're ready."

She nodded her agreement. "Courtney, I need you take her to the park in Pine Valley. Do you know where that is?"

"It's close to the town square, right?"

"Yes," she said. "I'll be there as soon as I can. Tell Audrey I love her."

Tears slid down her cheeks, and she disconnected. She rested her head against the back of the seat and stared out the window as Tucker barreled toward home. Hot dog carts and Audrey's favorite ice cream shop flashed by. How could everything beyond the horrors of the college be exactly the same as they'd been this morning? She closed her eyes, unable to handle the normalcy of the beautiful day.

For her, nothing would be normal ever again. She'd been shot at, terrified, and had stared into the eyes of death—into the dead eyes of Paul. A shudder ripped through her, and she blocked the image of the man who'd pestered her for months and was now on the way to the morgue. She couldn't allow herself to focus on what just happened or she'd fall apart. Once she got home, she'd give herself a few minutes to break down, then pull herself back together as she'd done before. Because her peace wasn't what mattered. She needed to be a safe place for Audrey, even if that meant pasting on a smile and pretending like everything was all right.

She'd been doing that for years anyway.

TUCKER STEPPED into the silent house behind Elizabeth, Otto trotting alongside him, and turned the deadbolt after closing the door. The hum of the refrigerator competed with the creaks and groans of the old, wooden floors. He'd never been inside her house. Why would he? He didn't deserve to be five feet from Elizabeth and her daughter, let alone inside their home.

Soft sunlight filtered through the window in the living room, highlighting a space filled with stuffed animals, coloring books and baby dolls. His chest ached as he pictured evenings spent with the two ladies cuddled together, watching a movie and eating popcorn. A life filled with love but missing one very important piece. A father.

A father he was responsible for getting killed.

"Thanks for letting Otto come in. I don't like making him wait in the car in this heat. Even if the air is running." He rested his hand on top of Otto's head and scratched behind his ears.

"No problem," she said with a frown, and refused to look in Otto's direction. Bending down, she picked up a teddy bear hidden underneath the couch and brought the plush toy to her nose and breathed deep. "I need to see Audrey. I need to get to the park."

Tucker nodded. "Grab a shower. Once you're cleaned up, I'll take you wherever you need to go. Then she can play while you give yourself a little time to process everything that happened." He didn't assume she still wanted him around but also couldn't bring himself to leave. Not when it looked as if the slightest breeze would send her crashing to the ground—when pain and sadness lingered in her hazel eyes.

Elizabeth stood and the teddy bear dangled from her grasp. "You don't have to stay."

He screwed his lips to the side and shoved his hands in his pockets. He wanted to wrap her in his arms, but he needed to remember the role he played in her life. Walls between them were high, and always would be, even if he'd do anything in his power to knock them all to the ground.

Rocking back on his heels, he shrugged and dropped his gaze to the floor. Elizabeth still wore her mud-caked shoes and black marks smudged the light carpet. "Do you want me to stay?"

Hesitation flickered in her eyes, but she nodded.

"Then I will. Go ahead and shower."

Elizabeth's shoes drifted out of his line of vision, and he hurried to the kitchen as he grabbed his phone and glanced at the screen. Two missed calls from Cruz. He pressed the call back button and sank onto one of the wooden chairs at the kitchen table.

"I found Lizzie," he said when the line picked up. "She was there, man. Saw someone get shot."

Otto padded in the room and laid at his feet.

"How is she?" Cruz's voice was loud in the absence of noise in the house.

Tucker propped his elbow on the table and dropped his forehead into his palm. "Shaken up. What the hell happened?"

"Sounds like someone started a fire to set off the alarm and waited until everyone was outside before taking a shot."

"How many fatalities?"

"Just one. My buddy on scene said they're looking into Paul Stevens. The crime scene reads like a personal hit on the guy."

"Must be his blood she has all over her." Tucker's voice shook. "Her shirt's covered in it. She's trying to be strong, but she's more than scared. She's traumatized."

"You still with her?"

"I'm not going anywhere until she tells me to leave."

A wave of silence pulsed over the phone. "You sure you can handle that?"

He cleared his throat and leaned against the hard chair. Cruz understood his long, complicated history with Elizbeth but that didn't mean he wanted to dive into that right now. He had a duty to be there for her. Period. It didn't matter what time spent with her did to him. "I got to go. We'll talk later."

Standing, Tucker pocketed his phone and hurried to the sink. No reason to let the stains linger on the carpet. Might as well get it cleaned up so Elizabeth didn't have to worry about it, and he could get her to her daughter as soon as possible. The paper towels and stain remover were easy to find under the sink. He crossed over to the living room in three easy strides. Besides, busy hands would help keep his thoughts off all the other shit stirring his mind. Even if it meant scrubbing mud.

With Otto glued to his side, he followed the trail of dirt from the front of the couch, beside the end table, and toward the front door. Scrubbing and cleaning, his hands moving furiously against the plush fabric—removing at least one stain that had been brought into Elizabeth's life today.

"What are you doing?"

Elizabeth's voice lifted his head in her direction. His gaze traveled from her pink-painted toenails to sleek calves and slim thighs fitted under a pair of frayed jean shorts. He coughed and forced himself to tear his gaze from her exposed skin and focus on her face as he rose, balling the soiled paper towel in his hand.

"You tracked in some mud. Cleaning it up is the last thing you need to worry about."

A hint of a smile pulled up the corners of her lips. "Thanks."

He swept his gaze across the carpet, making sure he'd cleaned all the dirty spots, before crossing into the kitchen to put away the cleaning supplies. "No problem." He glanced over his shoulder. Water dripped from the tips of her blond hair and no make-up covered the smattering of freckles across the bridge of her nose.

But she didn't need a damn thing to make herself more beautiful.

She pivoted, turning her back to the natural light casting a dim glow in the living room.

Wiping his hands on the back of his jeans, he faced her. "Ready?"

Elizabeth's chest rose on a deep breath. She scooped her long hair between her hands and used a rubber band on her wrist to tie the tresses on the top of her head. "Yeah. I won't calm down until I see Audrey. I know it doesn't make sense, she was never in danger, but the idea of something happening to me and not being here for her..." Tears welled in her eyes, and she shook her head. "I just need to hold her."

Tucker crossed his arms over his chest to keep from reaching for her. "You don't need to explain. Let's go."

He led her to the front door. Elizabeth couldn't begin the process of getting past the tragedy she'd witnessed today until she had her daughter by her side. He needed to reunite mother and daughter then leave them in peace. Healing would take time, but it would happen. Elizabeth was strong.

And unlike with the tragedy of his past, she wasn't responsible for someone's death. No matter how much time went by, healing would never happen for him. Gary's ghost would never allow it.

3

Elizabeth's flip-flops slapped against the ground as she rushed toward her daughter. Her heart raced with each step. Tucker matched her stride, Otto by his side, as she hurried past the sweet-smelling flowers dotting the pathway. The red spiral slide came into view, and Elizabeth jogged until the brick sidewalk gave way to the small wood chips that spread underneath the play equipment.

"Mommy!"

Elizabeth's heart lodged in her throat, and she swiveled in the direction of Audrey's sugary voice. A plethora of emotion pressed against her lungs, making it hard to draw in a breath, but that was fine. She needed her daughter in her arms more than she needed air.

Audrey raced toward her, her blond pigtails flapping behind her head and a wide grin plastered on her beet-red face.

Elizabeth crouched and flung her arms wide. Audrey's small, familiar body slammed against her, and her butt hit the ground. She engulfed her in a hug and sank her nose in her neck, inhaling the scent of sweat, sunscreen, and lavender lotion. A laugh bubbled up from her throat, and she molded Audrey to her.

Elizabeth caught a glimpse of Courtney rising from a bench at the edge of the playground. She lifted a finger, halting Courtney's motion toward them. She'd tell Courtney everything soon, but right now she needed a moment to just be with her daughter.

Audrey buried her head against Elizabeth's shoulder and damp clusters of hair smeared against her skin. Elizabeth didn't mind.

Leaning back, she framed Audrey's heart-shaped face with her palms and studied the dirt smeared across her cheek. "You're a mess, girl."

Audrey giggled and the sound made Elizabeth's heart sore higher than the robins sweeping across the blue sky. "No, I'm not. I'm hot."

Tucker's rumble of laughter had Elizabeth tilting up her head. The rays of sun highlighted the blond streaks in his short hair. Why was he still here? She was grateful for the ride to the park, but she hadn't needed an escort. Now that she and Audrey had a way home with Courtney, she wanted him gone.

At least that's the lie she told herself.

He bent forward and gently tugged one of Audrey's pig tails. He smiled at her face, pink and sweaty from playing in the sun. "Did you paint your face red or what?"

Audrey crinkled her nose. "Why would I paint my face red? And who are you? Is that your dog? Can I pet him?"

Elizabeth stood and rested Audrey on her hip, not wanting her near the animal. "Honey, this is Tucker. One of Mommy's friends." Audrey's legs dangled past her hips and the toes of her tennis shoes butted against her knees. She pressed the tip of her nose to Audrey's and savored the weight of her daughter in her arms. "Audrey could be in the sun five minutes or five hours and she'd be red as a beet."

A quality she'd inherited from her father, a thought that possibly came to Tucker as well. But she didn't want to dwell on the past right now.

Audrey strained against her grasp. "Can I play more?"

Fighting the urge to hold tighter, Elizabeth set Audrey on her feet and watched her sprint back to the playground, casting one quick glance over her shoulder at the lab mix who sat patiently at his owner's side. An ache shot out from Elizabeth's chest and encased her entire body, but she couldn't hold her back from playing any longer or Audrey would sense her unease.

Courtney stood glued to her spot, her hand covering her mouth as her gaze stayed fixed on Elizabeth. The need to know what had happened clear on her face.

Unable to put it off any longer, Elizabeth dragged in a deep breath. Reliving her nightmare wouldn't be easy, but she needed to let Courtney know everything.

Making her way across the mulch, Elizabeth spared Tucker a glance and wished she could see behind his dark aviator sunglasses. The shock of him showing up at the school had worn off and curiosity had taken its place. His insistence at staying by her side had a million questions raising to the surface—questions she wasn't sure she wanted answered.

Tucker and Otto kept pace with her as she weaved around running kids and slid by multi-tasking moms dividing their attention between multiple children and their phones.

Courtney stood in front of a bench with her lips tucked so hard inside her mouth, only a thin line of nearly white skin showed. Fear radiated from her red-rimmed eyes, and she darted her gaze from Elizabeth to Audrey as if afraid to take her eyes off either of them.

As soon as Elizabeth stepped into the shadowed comfort of the oak trees, Courtney grabbed her arm and pulled her into a hard hug. "Thank God you're safe."

Elizabeth leaned into her friend for a brief second, then skirted around Courtney so she could keep an eye on Audrey swinging on the monkey bars. "I'm okay. Thanks for bringing Audrey here."

"It's the least I could do." Courtney looped her arm through Elizabeth's. "Do you need anything else? Are you sure you don't want to rest at home while the little munchkin gets out all of her energy?"

Elizabeth took a step back until the backs of her knees hit the hard wood of the bench, then sank down. No way she would leave Audrey right now, but her limbs still strained to hold her upright. "I want to be with her. I'm fine."

"I can stay over tonight," Courtney said, tucking a strand of brown hair behind her ear. "Whatever you need. I'm your girl."

Elizabeth was torn between gratitude and frustration. As much as she appreciated her friends stepping in and being by her side, the more they consoled her, the more she'd fall apart. If she wanted to hold herself together for Audrey's sake, she needed to stand tall and not allow herself to lean into anyone's comforting arms.

She cut her gaze to Tucker and glanced up the tanned, chiseled arms crossed over his broad chest. Black ink circled his biceps and dipped under his shirtsleeves in an elaborate pattern. His hands could do a lot more than comfort her.

Heat crept into her cheeks despite the cool shade. She shook her head and trained her eyes on Audrey now running along a patch of grass with a group of children. Where in the world had that thought come from? Being with a man was the last thing she should be thinking about, especially Tucker. He was on the no-fly list, no matter how her body always hummed with excitement when he was near.

Which was why she needed to keep her distance. Tucker's actions had destroyed her family and taken away her one shot at happiness. No matter what happened in life, she could never ever forget that.

TUCKER TAPPED his index finger against his bicep and kept his eyes on the little blond pixie as she leapt and bounced all over the damn place. A quiet whine hummed from Otto's throat and his body shook as he controlled himself from running into the fray. Tucker loved kids but having them pop out of covered slides and scream at the top of their lungs as they ran after God knew what spiked his blood pressure.

Heat beat against the back of his neck, but he couldn't sit and relax beside Elizabeth and Courtney. The events of the day had him on edge. He should return to the retreat—he had a strict schedule to adhere to between the dogs' routines and therapy sessions—but the need to do something pulsed through him. And if keeping an eye on Audrey so Elizabeth could confide in Courtney was the only available task, so be it.

Besides, he hadn't laid eyes on Audrey since she'd been an infant in her mother's arms—a brief and unwelcomed visit to the hospital after she'd been born. He saw so much of Gary in her, it took his breath away. The way her face turned bright red in the heat, the curve of her chin, the dimples that flashed when she smiled—all inherited from a father she'd never know.

His phone vibrated against his thigh, and he dug it out of his pocket just as Audrey jumped from a platform with arms wide open, like a bird in flight. He winced and took a step forward, but the girl landed on her feet and ran off with a grin splitting her adorable face. The little gap between her two front teeth stood out, and he couldn't help but smile. That was definitely a feature from her mother. One he hoped she'd never try and erase.

He cast a quick glance at his screen before answering. "What's up, Cruz?"

"Sorry, dude, but wanted to give you a heads up. Looks like Paul Stevens was into some bad shit. Cops want to interview Elizabeth about their relationship."

He twisted away from the women and hunched over the phone, trying to ignore the shrieking kids in the background. "What do you mean their relationship?"

"Cops found some stuff Paul'd written down about Elizabeth. They want to find out how well she knew him. Looks more and more like a personal hit. If the bastard hadn't died, he'd be taken in for tax evasion, money laundering...and kiddy porn." Cruz gritted out the last two words.

Lead pooled in Tucker's stomach, and he rubbed his hand over his buzzed hair. "Shit. Didn't take long to uncover all his dirty little secrets."

"Main detective on the case knows me. He's filled me in on everything. They just need to tie up loose ends, see if Paul said anything to her over the past year."

Tucker cast a quick glance toward Elizabeth and Courtney. The women huddled together, their heads ducked low as they talked. "She won't want her daughter around when she talks to the cops. I can take her to the station if that'll be easier."

"Ask her and call me back. I'll set it up."

"Okay. Thanks." Tucker disconnected the call and swore under his breath. Elizabeth didn't need to deal with any more stress today, especially to answer bullshit questions. But if the police could tie more people to the crimes Paul committed, maybe some criminals could be put behind bars where they belonged.

Crouching low, he stared into Otto's eyes. "Stay and watch her, boy." He pointed at Audrey as she ran around like a hellion, and Otto barked once and kept his gaze locked on her.

Tucker stood and approached Elizabeth, twigs snapping

under his sneakers. Elizabeth tried to appear calm, but the emotion clouding her hazel eyes told him a different story. Courtney didn't even try to conceal the worry etched around the fine lines of her full lips.

"Cruz just called. The police uncovered some details about Paul Stevens they need to investigate. Part of that includes speaking with you. Do you want me to take you to the station, or would you rather they meet you at your house?"

Courtney's chocolate brown eyes bored into him, and Elizabeth pressed the tips of her fingers into her closed eyes as she rubbed circles into the sockets.

"Let's just go to the station and get this over with," Elizabeth said. "Do you have Audrey, Court?"

"Yes, don't worry about us. Go get this done, then you can put it all behind you."

The sound of Otto's fierce growl followed by continuous barking made the hairs on the back of Tucker's neck stand at attention.

Courtney leaned to the side and used her hand to shield her eyes as if it'd help her see into the growing crowd of children on the playground. "Audrey's on the other side of the playground. She's talking to someone I don't recognize."

"What do you mean?" Elizabeth spun around, rocking back and forth in search of her daughter.

Tucker's heart picked up speed. He roamed his gaze over the head of kid after kid, searching for the blond pigtails, but he couldn't find Audrey. "I don't see her."

Courtney shook her head, confusion rippling across her smooth brow. "She was just there. Where could she have gone?"

Elizabeth took off toward the playground. "She always stays where I can see her. She never walks away from the play area. Never would go anywhere with a stranger." Her words flew from her mouth in rapid succession.

"Audrey!" Courtney ran through the chaos of kids, turning

small children to face her, distress quickening her pace as she waded through the playground.

"Otto! Find her!" Tucker commanded.

The dog shot forward.

Panic thundered through him and eclipsed the yelling kids and chattering moms. He ran around the edge of the mulched in area containing all the play equipment, keeping one eye on Otto. A black wrought iron fence kept the children within its walls, but two entrances rooted either side. Courtney frantically looked for Audrey at one end while Elizabeth continued to search the interior of the space. He needed to get to the opposite end...and fast.

Tucker reached the far side of the playground. Most of the equipment sat on the other side. An open patch of green grass took up this part of the park and a handful of kids chased each other. None of them were Audrey.

Otto was ten feet ahead of him and zipped around the corner of the fence. He charged toward the street, and Tucker's heart lodged in his throat. Had he just sent his retired K-9 into action when he wasn't capable, again? The first time he'd made that mistake, he'd gotten his partner killed. This time, even more was on the line.

Gary's daughter.

A shriek sliced through the chaos of whooping screams and playful banter, and the flash of a blond pigtail invaded Tucker's vision. He sprinted forward just as Otto leapt in front of an older woman with Audrey's hand securely tucked in hers.

4

"Stop her! That's not her child!"

Tucker's frantic scream crashed into Elizabeth's brain, and she turned in a wide circle to find him. Standing on her tiptoes she searched past the crowd of playing children and spotted Tucker running toward the street. She scanned the gawkers staring at Tucker with wide eyes and opened mouths and spotted an old woman gripping Audrey's hand in hers.

Otto crouched low in front of her, teeth bared.

Tucker sprinted forward, pushing people out of his way as he barreled toward the street.

Terror rained down on her like one icy bucket of water after another, with no time in between to catch her breath. She broke into a sprint, ignoring the grunts of annoyance as she shoved past anyone in her way. "Audrey!" She yelled her child's name with a frenzy of fear and frustration she'd never felt before.

Footsteps pounded behind her, but she didn't spare a second to turn around.

Tucker reached the woman who'd snatched her child, and

secured Audrey in his arms, keeping one hand on the old woman's shoulder to pin her in place. Otto stood his ground, a menacing snarl twisting his face.

Audrey's wide eyes searched for her, and she quickened her pace, her arms outstretched as she reached Tucker and swiped her daughter from his grip. "I got you, honey. Mommy's here."

Audrey's little limbs trembled, and she buried her face in the crook of Elizabeth's neck. Tears flowed over her skin, and Audrey tightened her arms so hard around her throat it nearly choked her.

"You're okay, sweet girl. I've got you." She smoothed her palm over her back and made a shushing sound against her ear. She hated seeing her daughter so scared, especially when it was clear Audrey didn't understand what had even happened, but a part of her wanted to tuck her safely away then throttle the stranger in front of her. But she had to remain calm so as not to upset Audrey even more.

Tucker kept a firm hand on the woman's shoulder and held his phone with the other. "Otto, sit. Stay," he commanded as he swiped his thumb over the screen and pressed the device to his ear.

The woman pulled on the ends of her long, gray hair and darted curious blue eyes around as if unsure of why everyone was so upset. "I'm so sorry. I don't know what I did. Why are you mad? I just did what he asked me."

Her jumbled words sent spikes of panic through Elizabeth's chest. She noted the dirt smeared across her cheeks and worn clothing. Deep wrinkles lined her sun-kissed face, but she appeared to have her wits about her despite the nonsense she uttered.

"What do you mean? Who asked you to take my daughter?" she asked, straining to keep her voice even.

The woman fixed her gaze on Elizabeth. "Her father."

The statement nearly knocked her off balance.

Tucker set his jaw, and a jolt of pain flashed in his blue eyes. "Where is he now?" He held up a finger, asking for a second, before his focus returned to his call. "Cruz. We have a situation at the park," he said into the phone. "I need you here now."

"I don't understand. Why is everyone upset?" The woman knitted her hands in front of her waist, keeping her fingers in constant motion.

Indecision bounced around Elizabeth's brain. The mother in her wanted to run away with Audrey and never looked back. But the profiler in her wanted to talk to this woman who'd clearly been used for nefarious reasons—reasons that centered around taking her child. And both the profiler and the mother needed answers.

Courtney appeared at her side and rested a hand on Audrey's arm. "You've had quite the day, little one."

Audrey lifted her head. "I want to go home."

Elizabeth shifted her on her hip and offered the most authentic smile she could muster. "I need to talk to this lady for a second. Can you sit with Courtney? Right there on that bench where I can see you?" She dipped her chin toward a wooden seat that lined the pathway outside of the play area.

"I want the puppy with me," Audrey said on a soft whimper.

She fought the urge to cringe. She didn't trust dogs, especially Otto, but he'd just assisted in stopping the woman who'd tried to steal her daughter. That might not erase everything that may have happened to cause her mistrust, but she couldn't deny Audrey something that could comfort her. "I'm sure that could be arranged."

As if the dog understood—man that was disconcerting—Otto trotted to Courtney's side.

Elizabeth swallowed the anxiety that told her to keep her firm grip on Audrey, instead setting her on her feet and placing a kiss on her soft cheek. "Stay with Courtney. Promise?"

Audrey nodded, then looped an arm over Otto's neck.

Otto swiped his large tongue over Audrey's face, and she giggled. The sound loosened the knot cinching Elizabeth's stomach, and a little bit of stupid resentment she held against the animal melted away.

Tucker disconnected his call and shoved the phone in the front pocket of his jeans. "Cruz is on his way. Ma'am, we'll need you to stay here with us so you can answer some questions."

She nodded. "Okay. But I still don't understand what's going on."

Elizabeth forced herself to think beyond the frantic pounding of her heart that refused to slow down despite the fact danger had passed and Audrey sat on the bench five feet away. "Ma'am, can you tell me your name?"

"Bonnie," she said, licking her thin lips. "I didn't hurt her. The girl. I was taking her to the ice cream shop. I did him a favor."

"And why would you do someone a favor? Did the girl's father explain why he couldn't get his daughter himself?" The words burned as she said them.

Bonnie shrugged and shifted her gaze to her tattered shoes. "He had an emergency pop up. Said he'd pay me to keep an eye on his daughter then take her to the shop. I was helping."

"Where is the man now?" Elizabeth asked. "Is he here?"

"No." Bonnie finally stopped the movement of her hands and stared up at her with wide eyes. "He left. He said he'd meet us there."

"Do you remember what he looked like?"

Bonnie swished her mouth to the side as if giving the answer considerable thought. "Taller than me. He wore a black baseball hat, pulled low over his face. I couldn't really see his eyes."

"Facial hair?" Tucker asked.

"I...I don't know. I'm sorry. My eyes aren't the greatest, and I wasn't paying attention."

Elizabeth stared above the woman's mess of hair and locked eyes with Tucker, whose narrowed gaze and angry stance exuded authority.

"I'll head across the street and see if anyone's at Cutie's Creamery. It's the only place nearby that sells ice cream," Tucker said. "Keep her here. Cruz will want to talk to her."

She watched Tucker take off at a jog, her nerves a tangle of knots threatening to strangle her. But she couldn't let that stop her from getting to the bottom of what had just happened.

"What's going on? Am I in trouble?"

A slice of pity ran through the river of emotions drowning her. Whoever was behind this had used a poor old woman's weaknesses for his own gains, and nearly stolen Elizabeth's entire world. Bonnie wouldn't be able to tell them much more, and Elizabeth didn't want to be responsible for causing even more problems for the woman, but she needed to understand what she'd just been a part of. What she'd almost been an accessory to. "Bonnie, you just tried to kidnap my daughter. Her father didn't approach you today."

Bonnie lifted a trembling hand to her mouth. "Are you sure? Maybe her father showed up without you knowing. Maybe this is all a big misunderstanding."

Elizabeth frowned and shook her head. "That's not possible. My daughter's father died when I was five months pregnant. Whoever approached you lied and used you to take her. You'll need to speak to the police when they arrive."

Bonnie's head fell forward, and she dissolved into tears.

TUCKER KEPT one eye on Otto and Audrey as they played on the floor of the lodge at Crossroads Mountain Retreat. Brooke, the owner of the retreat and his close friend, had brought out sweets from the kitchen and sat on the floor with the adorable duo, trying her best to keep the girl entertained.

Most of his attention stayed trained on Elizabeth, who sat hunched over her knees on the brown suede sofa in front of the large fireplace, the stone hearth raising three stories to the wooden beams extended across the pitched ceiling. "Can I get you anything? Water? Coffee?"

She shrugged then fell back against the plush cushion. "Can you rewind the day so I can make sure none of this ever happened?"

Her answer pulled up the corner of his mouth. "Sorry. I would if I could." He kept on his feet, legs planted hip-width apart on the burgundy rug and arms folded across his chest. Audrey was safe here, but he couldn't help but stay vigilant.

Cruz took the oversized chair adjacent to Elizbeth, the breathtaking views of the lush mountain peaks on full display in the floor-to-ceiling windows behind him. He held a narrow notepad in one hand, a pen in the other. A shadow of scruff lined his normally smooth jaw and blue eyes were bright and alert. "Since time traveling isn't an option, are you ready to discuss everything that happened today?"

She sighed. "Might as well get it over with. Thanks for letting us come here, by the way. I didn't want to take Audrey to the police station, and I'm not ready to let her out of my sight."

"No problem," Cruz said. "We want to make you as comfortable as possible. Especially since you're a friend of Tucker's, not to mention the way you stepped in and helped Chet."

Tucker winced at the mention of his friend and chef at Crossroads Mountain Retreat. The reappearance of a serial killer a few months before had sent Chet on a spiraling path of danger. Elizabeth had agreed to step in and act as a profiler to help find the killer, something that couldn't have been easy for her.

She offered Cruz a small smile. "I'm glad I could help. I just didn't expect to be back in Pine Valley so soon with my own host of troubles."

"I'll do whatever I can to get rid of those troubles," Cruz said. "I don't have a lot to go over with you. Just some follow-up regarding what happened at the park and a few questions about Paul Stevens."

She clenched her hands in her lap. "Okay."

"There was no man who matched the description given by the woman at the park at the ice cream parlor or anywhere near the vicinity."

Tucker fisted his hands at his sides as Cruz explained their inability to find the man who'd tried to kidnap Audrey. He still couldn't believe Elizabeth had let the woman go. He understood the woman had been used, but she needed to understand she'd almost made a catastrophic mistake, and that meant consequences.

But not for Lizzie.

She'd understood the position the woman was in and didn't want to add to her troubles. She just wanted the man behind the whole charade found, and yet again, Tucker had failed her.

"I'll look through the limited security footage from the businesses downtown, but since no cameras are near the park, I'm not expecting to find anything."

Elizabeth pinched the bridge of her nose and practically wilted on the spot. "I know the drill, but let's hope luck is on our side."

"I'll let you know if it is." Cruz shifted on the chair, leaning forward as if wanting to gain a better read of her. The movement had Tucker on alert, and he held his breath to hear every second of conversation. "How well did you know Paul Stevens?"

She blinked at the change of subject. "Umm, not well. He was the chair of the department I work in at the college. He hung around a lot, always asking me out and trying to get me alone."

Tucker saw red but kept his opinions to himself. He hated the idea of any man sniffing around her, let alone someone who'd been into the bad shit Paul had.

"Were you aware of any of the criminal activities he was involved in?"

Her mouth fell open. "Absolutely not. We didn't talk about much. Most of the time it was me trying to get away from him. But criminal activities? Wouldn't the school have known about that?"

Cruz shook his head. "He didn't have a record, but the police uncovered some disturbing things while looking into him. Your name came up."

She reared back her head. "Mine? How so?"

Cruz flipped a few pages in his notepad and cast a quick glance at the paper. "Mostly notes with plans. Date ideas. Your teaching schedule. The officer who's in charge of the case at the college wasn't sure if you were in a relationship with him, or if Paul was trying to establish something."

She shuddered then ran her hands up and down her arms. "Definitely not a relationship. I'm sorry he was killed today, but the idea he was keeping notes about me is creepy."

"Agreed," Cruz said. "The police at Elm Ridge just wanted to make sure you weren't associated with any of his friends or...accomplices."

"No. I don't know any of his friends. Like I said, I tried to spend as little time with him as possible. Do the police think Paul was specifically targeted at the college?"

Cruz pressed his lips together and nodded. "Looks that way. Not only was no one else shot, but the shooter didn't even attempt to take down anyone else. Tracking whoever had a beef against Paul will hopefully send the police to the shooter."

Something nagged at Tucker, and he couldn't help but voice his concerns. "What are the odds that a man who was trying to date you was murdered the same day a man claiming to be Audrey's father attempted to have her abducted?"

She winced and her gaze cut to Audrey. "Not high. But what does that mean?"

Tucker ran his hand across the back of his neck, wishing he had an answer. "It means you need to be careful."

As if sensing the tension, Audrey jumped to her feet and scampered across the room, Otto on her tail. She climbed into Elizabeth's lap and curled against her. "Mommy, I want to go home."

Elizbeth wrapped her arms around the little girl and pressed a kiss to her head. "Are we done here?"

"Yes," Cruz said and stood. "I'll be in touch if I find out anything else. But I agree with Tucker. You need to be on high alert."

Brooke walked to Cruz's side, concern clear in her brown eyes. "I know you're more than capable of taking care of your-self and your daughter, but please remember, you're both always welcome here. We're all around if you need us."

Brooke's kind heart warmed Tucker down to his toes. He'd lost a lot in his life, but he'd gained so much when he'd found this place. Snatching his keys from his pocket, he shoved away all his doubts and insecurities about taking Elizabeth back home. The decision about where she stayed tonight wasn't up to him. "Ready?"

She nodded and climbed to her feet with Audrey still in her arms.

"Is it all right if Otto comes along?" He understood her resistance to Otto, but he hated leaving the dog behind. Espe-cially when Audrey seemed soothed by his presence.

Hesitation lit Elizabeth's face. "Sure."

With his tail wagging, Otto ran to Elizabeth's side and followed behind her as she walked toward the door.

The sight made his heart ache. At any other time, in any

other place, the picture could have been of a happy family without a care in the world. A mother, her daughter, and the family dog.

Instead, the woman that meant everything to him—a woman he could never have—carried her terrified daughter toward a home that wasn't safe beside a dog that had played a part in ripping everything away from her.

Somehow, Tucker had to find a way to keep them all safe, come hell or high water.

5

Tense silence vibrated inside the cab of the truck as Tucker searched for the right thing to say. Man, he hated what Lizzie did to him.

No, Elizabeth. She now despised him calling her by the nickname he'd always used. He had to stop thinking of her as Lizzie—the brilliant beauty who'd stolen his heart with a glance. She was Elizabeth, the woman his best friend had loved. The woman Tucker had let down time and time again.

Not wanting to be alone with his spiraling thoughts, he fiddled with the knob on the radio. "A little music okay?"

Elizabeth glanced over her shoulder for a beat and smiled before fixing her attention back out her window. "Sure. Just not too loud. Audrey's asleep."

He snuck a quick peek at the sleeping girl in his back seat, and his heart pressed against his chest. "She's had a tough day."

Elizabeth snorted. "That's an understatement."

More silence weaved between them, the soft sounds of an old country song filling the space. Damn, she made him feel like a teenage boy with zero confidence and no working knowledge of the English language.

"The town looks cute right now," she said. "Is something going on?"

He noted the quiet streets along the town square as he passed through and headed toward the highway. "Pine Valley always puts on a big fair for Founder's Day. All the shop owners decorate their window fronts and the town council lines up entertainment at night and food vendors. Rides and games will be set up Saturday and Sunday for the kids."

"Sounds like just the thing you'd hate."

He grinned. Sometimes he forgot how well she knew him. "I don't usually attend."

"Hmm," she said, as if not knowing what else to say.

The spaces between houses grew larger, the patches of trees lining the road more dense. The turn for the highway to Elm Ridge loomed to the right, and he took the exit, hating the fact that in minutes he'd have to drop off Elizabeth and Audrey and drive away. He tapped his finger against the top of the wheel, debating if he should speak his mind or not.

"What is it?"

"What do you mean?" he asked, arching his brow.

She rolled her eyes, and the hint of a smile curved her lips. "You've never been good at masking your emotions. You're nervous, which I get, but there's more. You're afraid to say something."

He barked out a laugh. "Anyone ever tell you what a pain in an ass it is that you can read people so damn well?"

Smirking, she shrugged. "All the time. But you're easier to read than most. I know you. So whatever's going on in that brain of yours, just tell me."

He blew out a long breath and merged into traffic. "I'm afraid to leave you and Audrey alone at your house."

"I'm a little scared myself, but what other option do I have? My parents are states away, and I don't have any siblings.

Neither did Gary. I mean, you were the closest thing he had to a brother."

The comment sliced through him like a knife. Not wanting her to see how much her words affected him, he cleared his throat of all the lingering emotion before he spoke. "What about Courtney? You two seem close. Could you stay with her?"

"She's in a two-bedroom apartment with her husband while they remodel a house they just bought. Wouldn't be ideal. Besides, Audrey needs normalcy. Routine. Not to be ripped away and whisked off to some place she's not comfortable."

"But your phone, your car keys, and whatever else you left behind is still in your office. Can you even get ahold of anyone if you needed help?"

She dropped her head against the back of the seat and faced him. "Good thing I have a landline, huh? Listen, I appreciate your concern, but we'll be fine. I can take care of us. I do have some experience and training when it comes to dealing with criminals. Not to mention there's no known connection between the two situations. Nothing concrete telling us that the person responsible for the shooting is the same man who tried to get his hands on Audrey."

The exit to Elm Ridge loomed ahead, and he slowed to slide onto the country road. "You can't really believe the two instances are completely unrelated."

"And how could they be?" she said, throwing her hands in the air as her temper rose. "Some madman with a gun took out a criminal in Elm Ridge at the college and hours later an unknown creep in Pine Valley uses an old woman to try taking a kid."

The hysteric pitch of her voice warned him to tread lightly. "I don't know. It's just a feeling I have. I don't want to not take this seriously and let something slip through the cracks."

"Trust me. I don't generally let things slip through the cracks where my daughter's concerned."

He nodded, understanding the topic was closed. He'd spoken his piece and now he'd just have to let things go. He had no right to even give his opinion where Elizabeth was concerned, let alone suggest she stay somewhere else for the next few nights until Cruz and the rest of the police force had time to find some answers.

The music changed and Audrey's soft snores lifted to the front seat as he turned onto Elizabeth's street and pulled into her driveway. He stayed on alert, making note of the well-manicured lawns and tended flower beds in the nearby houses. At first glance, the suburban neighborhood just a block away from downtown appeared a quiet, safe place to raise a family. But he wouldn't expect anything less. Elizabeth would have done her homework before buying a home to raise her daughter.

Shifting the truck into park, he rested his arm over the bench seat and twisted to face her. "Do you need help getting Audrey inside? I can carry her while you unlock the door."

Hesitation pinched her smooth brow before she nodded. "That'd be nice. Thanks."

He shut off the engine and opened the back door, waiting for Otto to jump down before unhooking the straps of Audrey's car seat and securing her in his arms.

A little moan escaped her mouth, and she wrapped her arms around his neck and snuggled closer.

Warmth spread through his entire body, and he soaked in the smell of sweat and the strawberry lollipop Brooke had snuck her at the retreat. He took a step back and Elizabeth swiped the booster seat from the vehicle, then made her way to the front door.

He couldn't help but admire the sway of her hips as she moved. In a different world, he could lay his heart at Elizabeth's feet and be there for her and Audrey every damn day.

But in this world, he had no doubt Elizabeth would stomp on anything he lay in front of her and demand his hasty retreat.

An order he was sure would come at any time. He was pushing his luck today, staying by her side as she overcame each dangerous situation that came her way. But any moment he'd be forced to walk away—leaving his heart with her once again.

At the door, Elizabeth unfastened the locks and swung it open. "You can just leave her on the couch. I don't want her to nap too long."

He dipped his chin then stepped inside, depositing the sleeping child on the sofa then dragging the pale blue blanket from the back of the couch and draping it over her shoulders. Otto laid on the floor, keeping guard. He stood, looking down at her and wishing he could be so much more to her than some guy she'd never met. A man with a million memories of the father she'd never know.

"I'm going to make some coffee. Do you want a cup?" She wrapped her arms around her waist, unease surrounding her like a heavy cloud.

He should say no. Should stop putting off the inevitable and head home. "Sure. One cup won't hurt."

She turned toward the connected kitchen, took a few steps, and stopped.

Her sharp gasp had him hurrying to her side. "What's wrong?"

She lifted a finger toward a bouquet of flowers in a crystal vase sitting on the marble-topped island.

"Those weren't here earlier," he said, frowning. Sidestepping her, he stormed across the tile floor and found a scrap of paper lying beside the vase. His blood boiled. "Whoever brought these in here left you a note."

"What does it say?"

He didn't dare pick it up in case prints were left on the paper, but he read the words aloud. "Sorry I couldn't unite our family today. Next time, I won't fail."

A CHILL SETTLED into Elizabeth's bones that couldn't be vanquished. She pulled the cardigan she'd thrown on tighter around her middle, but the soft fabric did nothing to chase away the goosebumps that had taken up residence on her arms.

"Anything missing? Anything else placed inside the house that doesn't belong here?" Officer Lincoln Sawyer spit out the questions from the doorway of her bedroom.

"No. Nothing." She trailed her fingers along the hard wood of her dresser, making sure all her trinkets and frames were exactly where they're supposed to be. "I just need to check my daughter's room."

She hated this. Hated this feeling of being violated in her home. Hated searching through her house, holding her breath with each turn because she couldn't be sure what she'd stumble across.

But most of all, she hated that she was standing in her bedroom speaking to a police officer she barely knew about how someone had gotten into her home without any signs of forced entry and left her a creepy message.

"I've dusted for prints in the kitchen and will talk to your neighbors to see if anyone has a security camera that could have caught the perpetrator breaking into your home."

She shuddered. "The door was locked when I arrived, and the locks were still in place on the windows."

"Anyone have a spare key?" He narrowed his blue eyes, and she could make out the hard set of his jaw under the beard.

She'd met Lincoln once before, when she'd worked on Chet Black's case, and his similarities to his twin brother still surprised her as much as the differences. Cruz and Lincoln might have the same shade of blue in their eyes, same face shape, and same broad muscular build, but Lincoln's shoulder-length hair was like a lion's mane compared to Cruz's close-cropped look.

"My nanny, and there was a spare in the kitchen that I grabbed when I came back from work earlier." Realization punched her in the gut. "Oh my God. I left my purse at work. Could someone have gone through the building and stolen my things?"

Lincoln frowned. "That's a possibility."

Her knees shook at the thought of someone rifling through her personal items then using her own keys to get into her home.

"Why don't you take a look in your daughter's room and make sure nothing else is missing. Then I'll talk to the neighbors while you figure out what you should do for the night."

Confusion furrowed her brow. "What do you mean?"

Lincoln used the tip of his pen to scratch behind his ear. "Staying here tonight isn't smart. At the very least, you need to get your locks changed. And chances are that won't be done before morning. At most, you should find somewhere to crash until the person responsible is found."

She drew in a shuddering breath and mentally flipped through her options. She hadn't been lying when she told Tucker she didn't have anywhere else to go, but Lincoln was right. Staying here tonight wasn't an option. "I'll check Audrey's room then pack some things for us if you want to check with the neighbors."

"Will do," he said, pressing his lips in a grim smile before disappearing down the hall.

She followed close behind, passing the lone bathroom she shared with Audrey and stopping in the doorway of her daughter's room. The sight of Tucker settling into the soft pink rocking chair, the dark ink of his tattooed arms shocking against the girlish fabric, forced a small laugh.

His head shot up. "What's so funny?"

She shook her head, not wanting to wake Audrey. After they'd discovered the flowers, Tucker had cleared the house and once they knew there was no threat still inside, laid Audrey in her bed. He'd been as vigilant by Audrey's side as the dog, who laid on the cream-colored rug beside the twin bed.

Taking a step inside, she studied her sleeping daughter. Her pink and white ballerina comforter was pulled up to her chin and she snuggled her favorite plushy—a round stuffed cat she called Kitty she'd gotten as an early birthday gift a few days before. The thought of displacing Audrey from her home made her uneasy, but the choice had been ripped away.

"I need to pack some things for her," she whispered and tiptoed to the closet. Best to let Audrey sleep until the last possible minute. Then she could come up with a plan that would be easy to explain without a million questions being hurled at her.

"Where will you go?" Tucker stayed seated in the delicate chair, leaning forward to rest his forearms on his knees. His broad, muscular body filled every inch of the dainty furniture.

Grabbing a bag, she shrugged. "Maybe a hotel for a couple of nights. Make it like a little getaway for the two of us."

"Sounds fun."

The clipped tone of his voice told her he didn't approve of her idea. She shoved some clothes and a few toys in the bag then stared at him. "What's wrong with that?"

"Nothing," he said a little quickly.

She hefted the strap of the bag on her shoulder and pinned him with her best don't-lie-to-me look that always made Audrey spill the beans. "Don't hold back. Not now."

He wiped his hands on his thighs then stood. "You'll be alone. Not to mention hotels have a whole host of issues when it comes to security. Whoever is making these threats is a sneaky sonofabitch. He disappeared after trying to take Audrey, knows where you live and managed to get inside undetected.

What's going to stop him from following you to a hotel and waiting in the lobby until he can get his hands on you?"

The day's horrible events laid out so simply sent a shiver down her spine and made it impossible to argue. "What other choice do I have?" She held her breath, waiting to hear his suggestion.

He scratched the early evening scruff that lined his sharp jaw. "Brooke mentioned you being welcome at the retreat. Why don't you take her up on it?"

A stupid flash of disappointment pulsed inside her. What had she expected? That he'd offer his own home? That'd be ridiculous, not to mention completely inappropriate.

But the retreat...that was an interesting suggestion.

"I'll leave you alone if that's what's stopping you from accepting," he said, lifting his palms in surrender. "I know I've overstayed my welcome today, showing up earlier and sticking to you and Audrey without being asked is crossing your boundaries. I'm sorry if I've made you uncomfortable. But Brooke wouldn't have offered you a place if she hadn't meant it, and I'll keep a low profile. I promise. I just want you both safe."

The earnestness in his eyes made the ache in her chest expand. She wished she could cross the room and burrow herself in his arms, soak up the strength of a man who cared about her, but that could never happen. Instead, all she could do was accept the option he'd presented then pray the man who'd chased her from her home was caught quickly so she could return.

"Okay," she said, then left the room to pack a bag for herself. She should say more, should explain that his presence today had kept her together. He'd been her rock, not a thorn in her side.

But she couldn't speak. A mixture of gratitude and regret lodged in her throat and misted her eyes. She'd kept Tucker at arm's length since Gary died, not once considering what he'd been through. The loss he'd experienced. She hadn't allowed herself to give him any more space in her brain than he already occupied. Doing so was a betrayal to the man she'd committed herself to. Even if that man was gone.

Because no matter how much time had passed or how much she refused to let herself think about Tucker, she couldn't deny the truth. Tucker occupied more than just a space in her mind, he occupied a piece of her heart.

Which was the very last place she wanted him to be.

6

With Audrey's hand firmly in hers, Elizabeth climbed the steps of the lodge at Crossroads Mountain Retreat and met Brooke on the wide, wrap-around porch. "Thanks so much for inviting us here," she said, still in awe of the magnificent log-cabin style building in front of her.

Brooke smiled warmly. "Glad I could help. Please, come in and I'll show you where you two will be staying." She grabbed the handle of the wheely bag Elizabeth secured in her other hand then led the way inside. "I thought you'd feel a little safer in the lodge instead of one of the cabins around the lake."

"Thank you. For everything." She urged Audrey along, allowing herself to take in the beautiful furnishings and craftsmanship of the building.

Earlier, she'd been too scared and in shock to appreciate the space Brooke had created. Warm mahogany planks lined the floor, interrupted by burgundy rugs to anchor the multiple seating areas spread across the open room. The stone hearth was at the center of the room, but the views at the far side of the lodge stole the show. A deck looking over the lake was attached to the back, visible through the window. The rockers and Adirondack chairs called for a morning cup of coffee to enjoy the magnificent mountains.

"It's the least I can do after everything you did for Chet and Mia."

"I didn't do much to help," she said, casting Audrey a quick glance. Her daughter was too young to understand what her previous career had entailed, and she didn't want to speak in front of her regarding the serial killer who'd tormented the chef and his assistant.

Brooke nodded in understanding and waved a hand toward a hallway on the opposite side of the front desk. "Feel free to explore anywhere you'd like and use all the facilities. The gym and pool are down that way." She winked at Audrey. "I hope you brought your swimsuit."

Audrey beamed and bounced on her toes. "Did you pack it Mommy?"

She chuckled, sure she'd be a prune by the time they left if Audrey had anything to say about it. "Sure did."

A squeal of excitement unfurled the coil of anxiety looped around her insides. Her situation might be far from ideal, but if she could make their stay a fun adventure, Audrey would never be aware of the danger surrounding them.

"Great! I expect to see you swimming then." Brooke turned in the opposite direction, passing by a wide staircase that climbed to the second and third floors. "The dining room is that way, therapy rooms and meditation spaces upstairs. The employee rooms are down that hall." She flicked her wrist a second time but didn't stop walking.

Elizabeth frowned. "Isn't that where we'll be staying?"

Fisting her hands on her hips, Brooke spun toward her. "No way. Those are no bigger than a dorm room. Perfect for an employee to crash for a night or two—longer if necessary. But not a good alternative for you and your daughter. You need more space. I have a few rooms in the lodge for guests who can't stay in the cabins, or even those who prefer not to."

A stab of guilt pinched her face. "No, I couldn't take one of those rooms. I don't want to mess with your livelihood."

Brooke held out a palm to stop her from rambling on. "I don't want to hear it. You're my guest. I plan to treat you as such."

"At least let me pay." She took a mental tally of her bank account. Staying at an extravagant resort geared toward improving the physical and mental wellbeing of law enforcement and veterans wasn't how she'd planned to spend her vacation budget for the year, but she could swing it. Especially if she was allowed to dive into all the different activities with Audrey. Who knew? Maybe it could even help her overcome some of her own mental blocks that had tied her down since leaving the FBI.

"No way," Brooke countered, rolling her eyes. She moved her head along with the motion and her long, chestnut ponytail swung back and forth. "End of discussion. Now follow me, please."

She worked on a more persuasive argument as she moved toward the place she'd be staying for the next couple nights.

Audrey trailed her finger along the wall as she moved, humming a tune Elizabeth sang to her on the nights she still let her rock her to sleep.

"Here we are." Brooke used an old-fashioned key to open a door, pushing it wide and letting them enter before handing off the key to Elizabeth. "I made sure to stock the fridge, but you can find anything in the lodge's kitchen. Chet runs a pretty tight ship, but he's a sucker for giving kids anything they want, and he's mellowed out quite a bit since the last time you saw him. Falling in love will do that to even the toughest men."

Sticking the key in the front pocket of her shorts, she quirked a brow. Chet had been gruff and a bit hot-tempered when she'd met him. Not like she'd expect anything less from a man who'd been through hell and found himself back in the middle of his worst nightmare.

"Thanks," she said, taking in the room. The studio-style apartment boasted a queen-sized bed with a colorful quilt shoved in one corner, a tiny kitchen with the bare necessities, and comfortable furniture centered around a smaller version of the fireplace from the front room. It was cozy and warm and just the right size for her and Audrey...even if she'd have to share a bed with her kicking daughter.

Audrey pressed herself against the back of Elizabeth's legs, one arm looped around Kitty. "Where's Otto?"

The question tightened Elizabeth's chest. She'd been grateful that Otto's presence had soothed Audrey, but she didn't want her to become dependent on an animal that wasn't hers.

Brooke crouched to Audrey's level. "Otto is with Tucker at the kennel. He likes to help Tucker take care of the other animals, and right now is dinner time for the dogs."

Audrey's eyes widened. "Tucker has more dogs?"

Brooke grinned. "Well, Tucker only has Otto, but the retreat has a lot of dogs we use for therapy. Dogs that are trained to help people feel good."

"Like how Otto helped me feel safe."

"Exactly."

Unshed tears stung the backs of Elizabeth's eyes. Audrey shouldn't need a dog to make her feel safe. She should never have been in a situation like this in the first place. Elizabeth had never felt like more of a failure as a mother, and it made her angry.

"Mommy?" Audrey asked, swinging her gaze up to meet Elizabeth's. "Can we go see the kennel? I want to help. Just like Otto."

She swallowed past the apprehension that nearly choked her at the idea of not just being around Otto, who she'd only made peace with today, but an entire building filled with dogs. But she couldn't deny Audrey. Even if she disliked the idea of her becoming more attached to Otto...and the man who owned him. "We can do that. But only for a little bit because it's not just dinner time for the dogs. We need to find something to eat, too."

Audrey hugged her tight then ran into the room and tossed her stuffed cat on the bed. She wiped her palms together then gave a little nod of her head, pigtails bouncing, then faced her. "All right. Let's go."

Elizabeth couldn't help but laugh at the theatrics then led her out of the room, getting directions to the kennel from Brooke as they retraced their steps. She'd appease her daughter, spend a few minutes at the kennel, then figure out how to keep Audrey busy so she'd stop wanting Otto around.

Because when Otto was around, so was Tucker, and Audrey wasn't the only one forming attachments that would lead nowhere.

EXCITEMENT VIBRATED from the dogs as they sat and waited for all their dishes to be filled. Most had kibble in their bowl, but they were trained not to eat until every dog had their dinner waiting in front of them. Tucker's dogs had to have their manners, as well as a few fun tricks for showing off. He hefted the nearly empty bag and filled the last dish. "All right. Eat."

A frenzy of wagging tails and drooling muzzles took over the individual stalls that housed the dogs. Each with their own beds and bone-shaped black mats in front of their wrought-iron styled enclosure that penned them in. All the dogs dove into their dinner except Otto, who kept pace beside him with every step.

Chet chuckled and shook his head. "You're mean."

"Nah, they love it." He folded the bag from the top and returned it to the storeroom before washing his hands and stepping back out into the main hallway.

A half-door separated the front of the building from the dogs, where a set of chairs sat clustered together and a counter held a computer that was mostly used for monitoring the animals. Chet sat on a stool behind the counter. "What's up with Otto? He already eat?"

Tucker ruffled the top of Otto's head. "He's on edge after today. Plus, he senses my anxiety."

"Hmm," Chet said. "Not too hard to sense that."

Tucker scowled. "I don't know what to do, man."

"About?"

"Elizabeth. Her and the kid staying here. Someone being after them. I mean, I can't just sit back and do nothing, but I also can't keep showing up. Attempting to be some stupid protector she doesn't want or need."

"You sure she doesn't want you around?" Chet nodded toward the large front window that looked out on the lake.

Tucker pushed open the swinging door, coming to a stop beside Chet. He stared outside, his heart sputtering at the sight of Elizabeth descending the grassy hill with Audrey clutching her hand.

"Looks like they're heading this way." Chet stood and clapped a heavy hand on his shoulder. "Maybe you don't need to be so worried about how this plays out."

The positive sentiment from his once gloomy friend made him shake his head. He was glad Chet had finally found happiness again after years of grief, but he still wasn't used to hearing anything besides one-word answers or a smattering of curses from the large lumberjack lookalike. "All I'm worried about is making sure they're both safe."

"Whatever you've got to tell yourself, man."

The door creaked open, and a riot of barking broke out.

"Quiet," Tucker said in a stern voice, and the ruckus died down.

"Otto!" Audrey ran in and threw her arms around Otto's neck.

The dog's tail wagged furiously, and he sat still as a statue while absorbing all the love and attention.

"I hope it's okay we stopped in." Elizabeth winced and kept one hand on the edge of the door. "Brooke mentioned you were feeding the dogs, and Audrey wanted to help. Like Otto." The last words made her smile spread wide, showing off the adorable thin gap between her two front teeth he loved so much.

"Perfectly fine, but I already fed them all." He glanced over his shoulder and noted all the dogs had gone back to gobbling their food.

"Oh, man," Audrey said, straightening but keeping a hand on Otto's back.

Chet cast a warm smile on the child, a hint of sadness lingering in his brown eyes, before focusing on Elizabeth. "Nice to see you again, but I gotta run. Dogs might have eaten, but time to take care of the humans. I'll see y'all later."

"Did you get settled?" Tucker asked.

"Yeah," she said, wrapping one arm across her middle and casting a nervous glance behind him. "Brooke is way too gracious. The room is perfect, and she encouraged me to use the facilities while we're here. It's almost like we're on a spa vacation and not something entirely different."

He chuckled. "Glad to hear it."

"Can I help you, Tucker?" Audrey tugged at the hem of his T-shirt and stared up at him with wide, hazel eyes.

"As long as it's okay with your mom."

Elizabeth nodded, although she didn't look convinced.

Then he remembered her fear of dogs and cringed. "They're all very well-behaved. Most are former K-9 dogs who were injured or lost their trainers. All are certified therapy dogs. There's no reason to worry about them around Audrey."

She rubbed her fingertip over the scar in front of her right ear. "I worry about everyone who is around her. Human and animal."

"I get that."

"So can I help?" Audrey slipped her small hand into his then turned her irresistible four-year-old stare on her mother.

He melted on the spot.

Elizabeth quirked a light eyebrow. "Depends on what Tucker has in mind."

"Well, after the dogs eat, they go outside. Sometimes I take them on walks, but most of the time, I let them work off some energy in their play area. Their favorite thing is chasing balls. How's your throwing arm?"

Audrey gave an exaggerated shrug and her lower lip jutted out, arms lifted in a W shape.

"How about we give it a try?"

"Okay! Come on!" She grabbed his arm and tugged until he had no choice but to follow along.

And he fell hard for another Gilmore girl, both more than capable of bringing him to his knees.

7

The muscles in Elizabeth's neck screamed as she waited for the water to heat for the crappy cup of instant coffee she needed to wake her the next morning. She rolled her shoulders forward then back, stretching her head from side to side, but to no avail. Sleeping with Audrey was like sharing a bed with a tiny torpedo, determined to cause as much destruction as possible.

Or in her case, to ensure her mother slept in the most uncomfortable position.

Not like she would have slept well anyway. Not when her mind spun a million miles a minute. After she'd pried Audrey away from the kennel and managed to get her to eat a few bites of dinner, it'd taken longer than usual to calm her down for bed. While Elizabeth had rubbed a soothing palm over Audrey's slender back, her body had been in tune with every creak and groan of the unfamiliar building. Each sound causing an explosion of possibilities to erupt against the backs of her eyelids.

But no matter how fast her mind worked or how many terrifying scenarios played out in her over-active imagination, she couldn't think of one person who could be responsible for crashing into her world like a wrecking ball. The only man who'd shown her any interest in the last year was dead.

The microwave beeped, and she opened the door to stop the obnoxious noise from waking Audrey. She poured the bitter-smelling grounds in the mug filled with hot water and took a small sip. Oh man, why in the world would someone choose to drink this stuff?

A soft knock sounded at the door, and she frowned. Speaking to anyone before her coffee was never a good idea, which was why she always made sure to wake up before her daughter, but she couldn't put off whoever had stopped by. Especially when it could be something involving the case.

She placed the mug on the counter for a beat so she could knot the belt of her robe then scooped it into her hands before padding to the door. A round peephole allowed her to see who waited on the other side, and she let out a small breath when Lincoln's face came into view.

"Morning," she said, swinging open the door. "It's awfully early for house calls, officer." She tried to make light of the situation with a small laugh, but Lincoln's pinched expression told her she'd missed the mark.

"Sorry 'bout that, but I didn't have another way to get ahold of you and I thought you'd like to know the building at the campus has been cleared. You can stop in at any time and pick up your things."

Relief sagged her shoulders. As hard as it'd be to step back on the crime scene, being without her phone had been more difficult than she'd expected. Especially now that she'd been ripped away from her home with no way to contact someone if needed. "Thanks. I appreciate you dropping by to tell me."

He shrugged. "No big deal. I came in with Brooke to grab a workout, then realized I didn't have a way to call you so thought this would be easiest."

"Good thinking."

"Do you have a way to get to Elm Ridge?" he asked, frowning.

She cringed. Her car was still where she'd left it yesterday in the faculty parking lot. Not to mention the thought of walking back on campus alone didn't sit right with her.

"Tucker's in the kitchen. I'm sure he'd give you a ride. Besides, it's not safe for you to be alone."

She tilted her head to the side, studying the scruffy beard and intelligent blue eyes. Had she gotten so bad at masking her thoughts, or could he just read her that well?

"Not to mention you'll find much better coffee in the kitchen," he said, grinning and tilting his head toward the mug in her hands. "Brooke keeps the cabins and rooms filled with the crappy stuff to entice some of the more reluctant guests to socialize."

Elizabeth snorted out a laugh and hot, grainy liquid sloshed over the side of her cup. "Does that work?"

"Worked on me." He winked. "If it's okay with you, I'll let Tucker know you'll be down soon and will need a ride. Take your time. He's schmoozing Mia into making cinnamon buns."

"And that's a bad thing?"

"It is on a Friday. Chet will have his head if Tucker messes with his schedule. But it's awfully fun to watch him try."

She couldn't help but grin as he left, and she closed the door. She barely knew the people who worked here, who lived here, and they'd all treated her with nothing by kindness. No wonder Tucker had put down roots in Pine Valley and chose to work at Crossroads Mountain Retreat. This place was warm and friendly and offered a type of security she'd always longed for—offered a sense of home and belonging she'd never known.

Audrey's soft grumbles stirred the quiet air, and she braced herself for what kind of child would awaken. Happy and vivacious or grumpy and not quite ready to wake?

"Mommy?"

The questioning tone brought Elizabeth to the side of the bed. She sat on the edge of the mattress and swiped a strand of blond hair from her daughter's forehead. "I'm right here, baby girl. How'd you sleep?"

Stretching her little arms over her head, she yawned. "Pretty good. Would have slept better if you'd have let me swim after dinner."

Laughing, she rolled her eyes. Not even awake a full minute and already pestering her to get in the pool. She'd put her off last night, citing the need to settle and bribing her with a movie and popcorn to end the evening, but Audrey wouldn't wait for long today. "I'm sure you'll get a chance to swim. But first, breakfast. Want to stay in your jammies while we run to the kitchen? I have to catch Tucker before he leaves."

Audrey shot out of bed and slid her feet into her favorite white bunny slippers. "Let's go."

Okay, happy and vivacious it was. As they walked down the hall toward the kitchen, she only hoped her daughter would be in just as good of a mood when she told her they'd have to take a little trip to the college.

To a crime scene.

Where a man had died.

She braced herself against the wave of turmoil that crashed down on her and led Audrey into the industrial kitchen located just off the dining room where they'd eaten dinner the night before. A hum of activity buzzed inside.

Mia, the assistant cook, swatted Tucker's hand as he reached into a giant silver bowl with chopped up fruit. "Get your grubby paws out of there."

Tucker laughed and plucked out an apple slice, popping it in his mouth before leaning against the marble countertop.

Chet chuckled and stirred a pot on the stove.

Lincoln poured coffee from a carafe into two mugs, offering her one with a soft smile.

A mixture of delicious aromas surrounded her. Sweet, savory, bitter—they all wove together to create a mouth-watering tapestry that made her stomach growl. She accepted the mug and took a sip, closing her eyes to enjoy the bold roast that made the instant coffee taste like mud. "God bless you."

"Glad I could be of service," he said. "I'm taking off. Let me know if you have any issues at the campus. Pine Valley Police Department is overseeing the investigation pertaining to what happened at the park, Elm Ridge is handling the rest of it. We're staying in contact with new developments, especially if they overlap."

She swallowed hard, grateful for Lincoln's discretion in front of Audrey. "Thanks."

He nodded, waved a goodbye to everyone else in the room, and disappeared out the door.

"I can take you, by the way," Tucker said. "If you want me to."

"I'd appreciate that. Once I get my purse and keys, I can grab my car and can stop depending on you so much."

A light blush stained his cheeks and he kicked at the floor like a child who'd been caught doing something wrong. "I don't mind."

Audrey skipped over to a stool tucked under the island that anchored the large room and climbed on top. "Where we going?"

"Mommy has to stop by work for a little bit. It won't take long."

"But I want to stay here." Audrey watched Mia mix gooey batter in a bowl. "What's that?"

Mia grinned. "I'm making muffins. Do you want to help?"

Tucker pushed off the counter and approached Audrey,

bending to mock-whisper in her ear. "Tell her you want cinnamon rolls and not muffins."

Audrey beamed and sat up straight. "I'd like cinnamon rolls, please. You should always say please," she said over her shoulder at Tucker.

Mia flicked her whisk toward Tucker and splattered cream-colored batter on his cheek. "You're sneaky."

"We don't have time for that anyway," Elizabeth cut in. Now that she knew she could get into her office and collect her things, she was anxious to get going. She needed to find out if someone had stolen her keys from her purse, or if there was another explanation as to how her house was broken into without leaving any clues.

"But Mommy. I want to stay and bake." Tears filled her eyes, and she blinked over and over to keep them from falling. "I'm hungry."

"We can bake later, honey."

"Pretty please."

The words came out on a slight pout that twisted her stomach. She was uneasy about taking Audrey to the college after what had happened yesterday anyway, now add guilt to the mix and she wished she could bury her head under a pillow and forget all her problems.

"She can stay here with us," Mia said, a hopeful gleam in her dark eyes. "I don't work at my restaurant in town today, and Chet's great with kids."

Chet's body went rigid for a brief second before he turned to face them, still stirring whatever was in the pot. "We'd love to have her around. Mia needs some help with the cinnamon rolls. Never makes them right." The smile buried beneath his beard gave away his joke.

Elizabeth softened, knowing the burly chef had lost his own child a few years back. "I wouldn't want to impose."

"No imposition at all. And you know..." Mia wiped her

hands on the front of her white apron and hurried to a narrow closet in the corner before returning with a scrap of material. "I even have a little apron to keep her nice and clean."

"Mommy?"

She couldn't deny the trembling bottom lip, even though the idea of leaving her daughter with people who she didn't know very well had her doubting her sanity. Audrey had almost been taken yesterday. How could she leave her?

But how could she take her to a murder scene?

Pivoting, Tucker caught her gaze and held it. "She'll be safe here. Safer than she'd be almost anywhere else in this world. Probably safer than she'd be with us." He raised his brows high, his message loud and clear.

Someone with a weird obsession had already gone after her once and broken into their home. Trotting Audrey around Elm Ridge, in broad daylight where Elizabeth's presence wouldn't be a surprise, wouldn't be the smartest idea.

"Okay. She can stay, as long as she promises to behave. We just need to be quick."

He nodded then stole another piece of fruit. "I'll put your coffee in a to go cup and we'll head out now."

She handed him her mug and prayed she'd made the right decision. If she didn't, and something happened to Audrey while she was gone, she'd never forgive herself.

8

The difference on campus between yesterday and today set Tucker's nerves on edge. The only sign something had happened in front of the building on the edge of campus was the strip of yellow crime scene tape caught between the branches of a towering maple. The parking lot was empty save from an old sedan parked in the handicap space in front and a beater truck in the far corner. No crowds clustered in groups with fear bright in their eyes. No emergency vehicles clamored in the lot.

But that didn't stop the prickles of unease from tickling the back of Tucker's neck as he ushered Elizabeth into the building.

"You doing okay?" he asked, keeping a diligent eye on each doorway they passed. The halls might be empty, no sound but the hum of electricity surrounding them, but that didn't mean someone wasn't lurking in the shadows.

She hurried her pace. "I just want to get this over with and get back to Audrey."

He'd reassured her again on the short drive that Audrey was in safe hands, then wracked his brain for ways to fill the awkward silences. But nothing seemed adequate. Nothing an appropriate topic of conversation.

So he'd turned up the volume of the radio and left her alone with her thoughts, his own brain working over a million questions.

He followed her into a dark room.

She flipped on the light and gasped. The stench of water-logged wood permeated the air, and tacked up posters crumbled off the walls, the paper ruined. "Everything's a mess."

"Where do you keep your things?"

"In the desk drawer," she said, making a beeline to the front of the room where her desk took up most of the space in the small office. "Thank God I sprung for the waterproof case for my phone." She plucked the device off a stack of soggy files. "I was too panicked to grab it before I ran out of here."

"What about your purse? Is it where you left it? I know it might be hard to tell, but does anything seem out of place?"

She sat in the ruined leather chair and cringed before leaning to the side to open a drawer. "Everything smells so musty." Straightening, she dragged the tan strap from its hiding spot and dropped the bag on her lap before rummaging through. "Keys are here. What does that mean?"

He shrugged, wishing he had a definite answer. "Someone could have found another way to get inside your house, or even made a copy of the key before returning it to your bag in hopes you wouldn't realize they had secured a way to come and go as they please."

She swallowed hard, fear widening her eyes. "Or someone already had a key and I never realized it."

The thought slammed against him like a sucker punch. He hadn't asked Elizabeth many questions about who might be responsible, and she hadn't offered any suggestions. But that was about to change. He needed to help, and he couldn't do that if he didn't know a damn thing about her life since they'd parted ways after Gary's funeral so many years ago.

"Is there anyone you can think of who would have access to your things without your knowledge?"

"No," she said, shaking her head. "None of this makes sense."

A deep sigh sounded from the doorway, and Tucker spun around to find a man close to his own age and a middle-aged woman staring inside the room with tortured expressions. His face was long and slender with a subtle curve around his chin, a day's worth of light stubble covering his jaw. Hers was round and full with high cheekbones and a sloping nose.

"I see your office didn't fare much better than either of ours," the man said.

Elizabeth rose and skirted around the desk. She folded the man and woman into her arms for a quick hug, then kept one arm wrapped around the woman's shoulders as she turned to face Tucker. "These are two of my colleagues. Sebastian Tillman and Lindsay Spencer."

He dipped his chin in acknowledgement and offered a grim smile. "Nice to meet you. I'm Elizabeth's friend, Tucker Clayman. Just giving her a ride so she could grab her things."

"That's so nice of you," Lindsay said, tears clouding her brown eyes. "No one should be here alone after what happened. Thank goodness for Sebastian. He walked me to my office and has stayed by my side while I searched for anything that's salvageable."

Sebastian gave a self-deprecating chuckle. "She thinks I'm doing it to make her feel better, when really, she's the one doing me a favor. I still can't believe Paul is dead. Have you heard anything?"

Elizabeth kept her lips pressed together and shook her head. "Not really. Just that he was the only fatality."

"It's so sad. I know he could be a bit of a pill, but no one deserves what happened. And to know the shooter is still out there..." Lindsay wiped at her eyes. "I was a nervous wreck all night."

"Same," Sebastian said. "Didn't sleep a wink. How's Audrey? Did she see the news or find out what happened?"

"I kept her occupied last night," Elizabeth said. "She has no idea what happened."

Tucker watched the exchange, intrigued by the dynamics at play and how Elizabeth interreacted with her fellow professors. The woman he'd known had been an outpouring of information and oozing energy. This Elizabeth was tight-lipped and a hard edge had taken over her features, a visible shield to everyone around her.

Was he to blame for that, too? Had the part he played in Gary's death caused her to clam up and keep everyone around her at arm's length? Or was this a reaction from yesterday's events?

"I'm glad for that," Sebastian said, rubbing his hand over his short crop of sandy blond hair. "Listen, if you're finished here, Lindsay and I are meeting some of the other faculty members at Freddie's Café. Just to chat or vent or whatever. You two are welcome to join."

Lindsay clutched Elizabeth's hand. "Oh, please say you'll come. Scott and Mindy and Ed will be there. Most of the department, really. A coffee salute to Paul might make us all feel a little better."

Elizabeth twisted her lips, clearly not convinced she should go.

He didn't blame her for not wanting to toast the man who'd been such a slimeball, but it was obvious the other staff members weren't in the know about the type of activities Paul was involved in outside of work.

But it would be interesting to hear what they *did* know.

"We have time," he said, fixing Elizabeth with a wide-eyed

stare, hoping she understood his intent. "It might help with some closure or healing to discuss Paul with those who knew him so well."

Realization brightened her eyes. "Good point. I just need to call Mia and ask if it's okay if she watches Audrey a little bit longer."

"I've got her number," he said, grabbing his phone and swiping it to life. "I'll shoot her a text and let her know what's going on."

He typed out a quick message then put Elizabeth's phone in the purse she'd left on her chair. "Do you need anything else?"

"No. That's everything."

A ding turned his attention to Mia's quick reply. "She said take all the time we need and sent a picture of Audrey with a giant cinnamon roll," he said with a laugh. "I finally got Mia to make me rolls on Friday and she reaps all the rewards."

Elizabeth grinned. "Sounds about right. She always has a way of getting exactly what she wants."

"Sounds like her mother," Sebastian said.

Elizabeth aimed a bemused look at her friend that caused spikes of jealousy to course through Tucker's body.

Following her out of the room, Tucker stomped out the lingering envy he had no right feeling. Elizabeth was among friends and coworkers and she could enjoy playful banter with anyone she liked. And hopefully that banter could lead them to some answers they desperately needed.

THE SNAPPING of bacon and scent of sweet pancakes reminded Elizabeth that she hadn't eaten anything since last night. Even then, she'd barely managed more than a couple of bites. Her stomach gurgled, and she pressed a hand against it. Maybe attempting to eat something wasn't the worst idea.

A smiling hostess stood behind a wooden podium with a stack full of plastic menus and let her eyes roam appreciatively over Tucker.

Annoyed, Elizabeth cleared her throat, snagging the hostess' attention.

Amusement lifted her brows. "Just the two of you this morning?"

"I see our table," Tucker said. "Thank you."

He molded his palm to Elizabeth's back and pointed out where her friends sat in a corner booth, then stayed close behind her as he followed her through the maze of tables. The heat of his hand singed her spine.

Crap, this wasn't the reaction she wanted to experience every time he was near. She obviously couldn't control her baser instincts, so she needed to find a way to put some space between them. And the only way to do that was to figure out who'd tried to take Audrey and broken into her house. It was time to stop pretending like she was just a professor. She was a profiler, through and through, and a damn good one at that. She'd need every single skill she'd honed over her years spent in the FBI to dive deep into the psyche of someone who was after her.

With her agenda in the front of her mind, she slid onto the booth beside Lindsay as Tucker grabbed a chair from a nearby table and placed it beside her, his back to the dingy cream-colored wall.

"So glad you could make it," Mindy said, aiming a sad smile her way. Her wrinkled hands rested on her lap and gray hair was pulled back in the sleek, low bun she always wore. "We all just feel awful about what happened yesterday. I still can't believe Paul's gone."

Elizabeth dipped her chin, agreeing it was sad for Paul to meet his end the way he did, but she couldn't find herself to be too sad that someone so awful would no longer be casting his long shadow over so many horrible—illegal—arenas.

"I'm sorry you all went through what you experienced," Tucker said, leaning forward. "Being in that situation is never easy, then for one of your coworkers to be killed. Were you all close?"

She bit back a smile. He was a police officer to the core, even if he no longer carried the badge.

A tiny hesitation pulsed through the group, speaking volumes, before Scott responded. "We all spend quite a bit of time together. Paul's position meant he kept tabs on all of us. Overseeing things and reporting to the dean, that sort of thing. In such a close-knit community like ours, it's impossible not to feel his loss."

If Tucker was half as good at his job as he used to be, the subtext wouldn't be too hard for him to decipher. Paul was an ass who held his authority above them all and used it for personal gains.

"Did you all hang out like this outside of work a lot?" Tucker asked.

Mindy shrugged. "Some of us grabbed dinner from time to time. Paul didn't usually come with us. Always said he was busy, except when Elizabeth came. And didn't you two hang out a little, Sebastian?"

Sebastian's shoulders tightened; his jaw hardened. "Not really. I hate to speak ill of the dead, but the guy was a jerk. I'm sorry about what happened, and I'm sure his family is gutted, but I can't say he and I were exactly friends."

The words sparked Elizabeth's curiosity. "Does he have a family?"

Sebastian shrugged. "Doesn't everyone? I mean the guy wasn't married or anything, but I'm sure he has parents or siblings or something. This will be tough on them."

She made a mental note to look into his home life. She'd

never given much thought to who Paul had spent his time with, she'd just wanted to stay as far away from him as possible. And honestly, it might not even matter. But she couldn't help but wonder if even from the grave, Paul was somehow connected to everything that had happened.

A brown-haired server with a plump face and kind eyes approached the table. "Y'all ready?"

Everyone took turns placing their orders. After Tucker asked for coffee, Elizabeth asked for tea and buttered toast, offering a smile to the young woman who often served her and Audrey when they stopped in to eat. Elm Ridge was a small town that didn't boast many options for dining out on the evenings she didn't feel like cooking.

Once the server walked away, Elizabeth focused on Ed hunched over the table in the corner of the booth. Although she hadn't gotten too close with any of her coworkers, she felt a kinship with Ed that came from a shared tragedy. He was also a young widower, although his wife had passed tragically after a battle with aggressive cancer. The broody-faced man who always seemed to wear a five o'clock shadow was forced into the single parent role, making him a source of constant crushes and interest to both faculty and students when he pushed his nine-month-old son around campus. "How are you holding up?"

He lifted the corner of his mouth, the dimples on his cheek deepening. "Okay, I guess. None of this feels real. I held Oliver all night long. I couldn't bring myself to put him down."

"I know what you mean." Her mind flew to Audrey, back at the retreat making cinnamon rolls with two people she barely knew, and her chest tightened.

Maybe she should skip breakfast and head back. As much as she'd like to focus on figuring out this maddening puzzle, concentrating on picking apart every word spoken by the people at this table proved impossible.

Instinct had her grabbing her phone and checking for any messages. She'd left Mia her contact information and didn't want to miss anything she may have sent. A few unread texts and announcements of unanswered calls showed. She swiped her finger across the screen then lifted it a fraction to unlock it with a brief scan of her face.

And her breath caught.

All the apps that normally clogged her screen were gone and the photo of a smiling Audrey from her first birthday had been replaced with a picture of the two of them. Her in a bridesmaid dress carrying a bouquet of flowers, and Audrey in her white flower girl dress with a crown of daisies around her head.

With shaking fingers, she turned the phone toward Tucker.

"What's wrong?" he asked, scooting to the edge of his chair.

"The picture. I didn't set it as my home screen. Someone tampered with my phone."

9

A sense of foreboding washed over Elizabeth. She stood in front of the Pine Valley Police Department, a brown brick standalone building just off the square, and waited for Tucker to park his truck. The last time she'd stepped foot inside, she'd jumped into the mind of a serial killer to help Chet and Mia. This time, the reason was much more personal.

Tucker turned the corner, a deep frown pulling down his full lips, and hurried to her side. "I wish you would have ridden with me. I was concerned before. Now I'm creeped out and pissed as hell. The whole drive here I kept looking in my rearview mirror, praying you were still there."

His concern warmed her cheeks way more than the scorching sun. It'd been a long time since she had someone around to worry about her, and she hated how much she liked it. "It didn't make any sense to leave my car back there. Now you don't have to keep driving me around."

He moved his jaw back and forth as if searching for the right thing to say. "I like helping you whenever—however—I can. It's the least I can do after everything."

She didn't know what to say or how to respond. He didn't owe her anything, but if she really believed that, why had she held onto her anger for so long? Why had she forced a distance between them that deep down she didn't really want?

The glass door to the station swung open, and Cruz poked out his head. "Want to step inside?"

She offered him a stiff nod and skirted around Tucker.

Cruz ushered them through the quiet bullpen where a couple officers hunched over their desks, busy with paperwork. He led them to his office, closing the door behind them before taking a seat.

"Thanks for seeing us." She sat beside Tucker, clutching her purse against her chest. Nerves danced in her stomach. "I know we could have called the Elm Ridge Police Department, but you're already looking into the park abduction and break in at my house. This issue seemed like it would fall to you."

Not to mention something about this town and the people in it made her just feel more comfortable, more secure in their ability to rally around her and help her with her problems. That might not be fair to the fine men and women working diligently in Elm Ridge, but she didn't care. Instincts were there for a reason, and she planned on following hers.

"I'm glad you called. And from what Tucker told me on the phone, this is more than an issue. This is breaking into a crime scene and tampering with your personal belongings. Now I have to ask, are you sure someone else put that photo on your screen?"

"Yes," she said. "No doubt."

"And was this a picture that was already on your phone?"

She nodded.

"Is your phone pass coded?"

Tucker had asked the same question after she'd made the startling discovery. She fiddled with the ends of her hair as their discussion came to mind. "Yes, and the code is my daughter's birthday."

Cruz's blue eyes widened. "Something tells me that's not a lucky guess on someone's part."

She cleared the fear from her throat. "I doubt it."

"Can I see the phone?"

Rummaging through her bag, she found the device and unlocked it before passing it over the desk.

Cruz studied the screen and frowned. "Except the sage colored dress you're wearing, you look like a bride here."

A shiver raced down her spine.

"Let me see that," Tucker said, voice tight and clipped.

"That okay?" Cruz asked, seeking her permission—which she gave with a dip of her chin—before handing it over to Tucker.

Tucker stared at the screen, anger twisting the muscles of his face. "You're right. I hadn't noticed that before. When's the picture from?"

She blew out a long breath. "Courtney's wedding in May. She's my nanny."

"So fairly recent," Cruz said.

Tucker studied the photo for another beat then returned it to her. "So what do we do? Her house was already combed over for clues and dusted for prints, and so was the crime scene at the campus. The phone was on top of her desk and drenched in water from the fire alarm. Not to mention had already been handled and thrown in her purse before we realized someone messed with it."

"Did you find anything else in your office that concerned you?"

"My house key was still in my bag, but that doesn't really prove anything. Someone was obviously in my office. The question is, would they have taken the chance of breaking in twice

—once to take the key and change the photo on my phone and again to bring the key back?"

"Are there security cameras on campus?" Tucker asked, clenched fists atop his thighs.

"Should be," Cruz said. "I'll call Officer Edwards. He's in charge of the investigation regarding the shooting. There should have been a patrolman keeping an eye on the crime scene all night as well, but with limited resources, that's not always the case."

Determination surged through her. "In the meantime, I'd like to take a look at the case files. I know everyone is doing all they can, but that needs to include me as well. I need to have a hand in this. I can't just sit around and wait for the next shoe to drop—the next twist to come. I want to work out a profile on whoever's behind this. Look at this strictly from a professional's point of view."

Tucker draped an arm around the back of her chair, as if needing to support her in some way. "With you being the person targeted, do you think that's possible?"

She shrugged. "I have to try. I mean, between my training and background, as well as probable knowledge of the person we're looking for, who'd be better for the job?"

Cruz flicked his gaze toward Tucker then back to her. "Sometimes when we're this close to a case, it can cloud our judgment. Make us miss things."

Tucker stiffened. "Lead us to make decisions we'll regret for the rest of our lives."

Sensing his need for comfort, she rested a hand on his knee until he finally looked her in the eye. "When you went after Otto that day, Gary and I both understood what he meant to you. We both knew why you couldn't follow the order not to storm into that building. You had to protect him, just like Gary had to protect you. He made his own decision to go in after you, knowing the building wasn't safe, and some asshole with a gun took his life. Not you."

Something loosened inside her chest as she finally recognized the truth. She'd blamed Tucker because she'd had no one else to blame. That hadn't brought Gary back; instead all her misplaced anger had done was riddle Tucker with guilt and kept him from being a part of her life.

He swallowed hard and sniffed back unseen tears.

"But this is different. Until I know who is after me and my daughter, I'm in the line of fire. I'm in danger. I have to do what I can to keep us safe."

Tucker gave a slight nod of his head, whether in acknowledgement to her finally offering words of absolution or in agreement to her plan she wasn't sure. But either way, something loosened inside her chest that had everything to do with helping wipe away a little bit of the guilt Tucker carried on his shoulders.

Maybe she'd been looking at their situation wrong the whole time. Maybe staying away from Tucker had only hardened the edges of her bitterness. Neither of them asked for the pain and grief they'd been burdened with. Separating herself from him hadn't lessened any of those feelings. Could it be possible that she'd made a mistake and the key to finally finding peace could be found with the man she'd avoided for so long?

WITH THE FILES regarding Elizabeth's case photocopied and placed in her purse, and a request put into the Elm Ridge Police Department to send their notes digitally to her email address, Tucker said goodbye to Cruz and walked her back through the building to the exit.

"I hate we were gone so long," she said, checking her watch. "I hope Audrey isn't upset."

He snorted. "Something tells me she's being pampered by everyone who sees her and she's loving every minute of it."

Pushing through the door, he welcomed the warmth of the sun on his skin. The air conditioning inside had been on full blast, and he hated sitting in the hard chair in Cruz's stuffy office. After working at the retreat for a couple years now, he craved the outdoors. Needed the open space and clean air to keep him centered—the companionship of his dogs to keep him grounded.

"I'm sure you're right. But I need to stop her fun, and I bet you have to get back to work."

He shrugged, wishing he could draw out their time together. "I have someone covering for me."

"Well, I guess I'll see you there." She smiled and turned toward the parking lot attached to the side of the police station.

He'd been forced to park down the street, opposite end of the square, and wasn't comfortable with her walking to her car alone. Even with its close proximity to the station. "I'll walk you to your car."

She flashed a quick smile. "Ok. Thanks."

He shoved his hands in the pockets of his jeans. "Will you dive into the case once we get back?"

"Hopefully. Depends on Audrey. I might have to wait until I put her down for a nap."

"Do you have any idea who could be causing all this?" he asked, unable to keep his questions to himself any longer. "Any guy you've dated recently who wanted to take things further than you did? Someone who's hung around you've thought a harmless nuisance? A friend who flirts or a barista at your local coffee shop who asks a lot of personal questions?"

Gravel crunched under her tennis shoes as she crossed the

parking lot to her small SUV in the back. "I haven't stopped thinking about this. Asking myself a million questions. Looking at everyone I can think of with suspicion. Not one person comes to mind."

Reaching her car, he waited for her to beep the door unlock then opened it for her. "I know you just got the files, but when looking at the surface, what does the profiler in you think?"

She bit down on her bottom lip, making the slight gap between her two front teeth more pronounced. "It's clear someone has an obsession. They know where I live, where I work, and how to access my phone. Which means they're aware of Audrey's birthday. The note left at my house screams delusion. The idea that we're a family he's trying to put back together is terrifying. Going through the files will hopefully help me narrow things down." She tossed her purse onto the passenger seat. "See you back at the retreat?"

The question warmed him to his toes. He'd assumed she'd want to be away from him as soon as she got the chance. He hated the reasons for her being at the retreat, but maybe the forced proximity could help heal some of their past hurts. No way he'd ever have Elizabeth the way he wanted her, but he'd take her friendship any day of the week. "Absolutely."

He waited for her to climb inside and pull out of the lot before retracing his steps back to the sidewalk. If she'd let him, he hoped to lend a hand. He might not be an officer anymore, but that didn't mean he couldn't still do the job.

His truck came into view and he hurried his pace, not wanting to be away from Elizabeth any longer than necessary. He fished his keys out of his pocket and unlocked the vehicle before reaching for the handle.

A hard blow to the back of his head sent him staggering forward. His ears rang and pain erupted in his skull. He fell against the truck and struggled to turn toward his attacker.

The sharp tip of a knife pressed against his back. "She's mine. Do you hear me? Mine! Stay away from her, or next time, I'll kill you."

Another hard punch to the side of his head had stars swimming in his vision, and he fell to the ground.

10

Hours may have passed since Elizabeth had left Audrey in the kitchen, but the scent of cinnamon and sugar still hung in the air. She stood in the doorway and grinned. Audrey's little apron was streaked with melted chocolate and dusted with flour.

Mia bent over the stove and pulled a tray of something sweet smelling from the oven while Chet stood beside Audrey, assisting her in cleaning up the mess of ingredients spilled over the stainless-steel island.

Elizabeth hoisted her heavy purse higher on her shoulder. "How in the world did you talk Mia and Chet into staying here with you for this long? You should have lunch and dinner prepared by now."

"Mommy!" Audrey tossed her white towel on the counter, hopped off a foot stool, and ran to her with open arms. "I missed you, but I made cookies and muffins and cinnamon rolls."

Laughing, she bent low and engulfed Audrey in a hug. "Then your belly must be pretty full. Sounds like nothing but fruits and vegetables for the rest of the day."

Audrey giggled and gave her one more squeeze before skipping back to the stool and continuing with her clean up. "Chet says if you're gonna cook, you're gonna clean."

Chet nodded and a hint of a smile cracked through his gruff expression.

"Don't worry," Mia said, swinging around to face them after placing a baking sheet filled with cookies on the stovetop. "We didn't let her eat everything we baked, and I gave her a yummy early lunch that was good for her."

"Thanks. For feeding her and watching her. We didn't expect to be gone for so long."

"We understand," Mia said. "And Audrey was a big help. We froze a lot of what we made for the weekend."

Chet wiped off the last bits of crumbs then frowned. "Where's Tucker?"

She hated the tiny knots that formed in the pit of her stomach at the question. On the drive here, she'd checked the rearview mirror a hundred times for Tucker's truck, but nothing. Not one sight of him. "I'm not sure. He walked me to my car, but I didn't see him on my way here. I called but he didn't answer. Maybe he had errands to run before coming back."

Chet scratched at his jaw. "Nah. He ran those the other day. Guy's a creature of habit. Not to mention Otto's been cooped up all mornin'. He hates that. Would want to spring him loose as soon as possible."

The knots tightened, and Tucker's words from earlier flitted to mind. He'd admitted to being nervous about her driving from Elm Ridge to Pine Valley alone and checking to make sure she was in view throughout the trip. It didn't seem plausible that his nervousness dissipated after speaking with Cruz. If Tucker was anything like her, the nerves would have only grown.

Mia rested a hand on Chet's shoulder. "I'm sure he'll be back soon."

"Can I spring Otto loose? I miss him." Audrey's bottom lip jutted out and a slight whine drew out her words.

As worried as she was about Tucker, she needed to focus on her daughter. Mia might not have let Audrey sample all the sweets, but the disruption to her schedule and more sugar than she was used to spelled disaster. She needed to get her back to their room and down for a nap soon before she lost it. Then she'd call Tucker again and find out what had kept him.

"As soon as Tucker gets here, I'll see when we can visit Otto. Maybe we can take him on a walk." She'd leave out the part about waiting until after a nap.

Audrey huffed out an irritated breath. "Fine."

"Let's head back to the room," she said, extending a hand for her daughter to grab. "Tell Mia and Chet thank you and we'll see them later."

She let her little face fall forward then jumped down and wrapped her arms around Chet's legs. "Thanks. Bye."

The look of joy and pain on Chet's face brought tears to Elizabeth's eyes and she dashed them away before anyone noticed.

After another quick hug for Mia, Audrey bounded over to her and clutched her hand. Elizabeth led her through the dining room and down the hallway toward their room. Her anxiety rose with each footstep on the carpeted floor, but she couldn't let it show. Couldn't let Audrey pick up on her feelings or she'd never calm her down to rest for hopefully a few hours.

"What did you have for lunch?" she asked, trying to stop herself from jumping out of her skin.

Audrey swung their joined hands back and forth as she waited for Elizabeth to unlock the door. "Turkey and cheese and yogurt with strawberries."

"Sounds good. I might have to have the same thing." She swung open the door and ushered Audrey inside before shutting it and engaging the locks. "But first Mommy is super tired."

Audrey frowned. "Why? It's so early."

"Yes, but I didn't sleep well last night. Some little peanut kept kicking me." She tickled Audrey's sides and she giggled, squirming away. "I need to rest for a little bit. Do you want to rest with me?"

"No," she said, scrunching her nose. "I want to swim. And see Otto." More whining, this time occupied with a tiny stomp of her foot. Which looked ridiculous with her bunny slippers still on.

Elizabeth sucked in a deep breath. Losing her patience wasn't an option right now, but man, with everything else pressing down on her, it was difficult. "We can't see Otto until Tucker gets back. If we lay down and rest for a few minutes, he'll be here before we know it. Then we can take Otto on a walk in the woods. Find some new trails to explore. Wouldn't that be fun?"

Audrey yawned and stretched her arms over her head. "Can Tucker come, too?"

Her heart lurched at the question. Audrey wasn't just getting attached to Otto, she was getting attached to Tucker as well. There was more than one way her daughter could be hurt at the end of this and being ripped away from those she'd grown to care about was one of them.

And the gnawing sensation in her gut told her Audrey wasn't the only one at a risk of getting hurt.

She coughed to clear her throat. "Sure, honey. If Tucker wants, he can come too."

Audrey smiled and pulled the apron over her head before tossing it on the floor and jumping into bed.

Rolling her eyes, Elizabeth scooped up the dirty fabric and placed it on the table. She'd won the battle of naptime so now was not the time to argue about good manners and cleanliness. She made a mental note to wash the apron before returning it to the kitchen.

She laid down beside Audrey and rubbed her back for a few minutes before her eyes fluttered closed and her breathing evened out. Elizabeth smiled. She knew her kid so well. Next year would be rough when Audrey started kindergarten and she'd been in school all day—no naps usually meant a very cranky Audrey. Even at almost five years old.

A sharp rap on the door had her bolting upright and hurrying to the entrance of the room. She checked the peep-hole and the sight of Chet's worried eyes and clenched jaw made bile slosh in her stomach. With trembling hands, she opened the door.

He didn't wait for her to say a word. "Tucker's hurt," he said, keeping his voice low. "He was attacked. Cruz found him beside his truck."

She gasped and her nausea shot up the back of her throat. "Oh my God. Is he okay? Where is he now?"

"He's awake. They took him to the hospital."

"I have to see him. Audrey's asleep. I'm so sorry to ask, but can you or Mia stay with her while I'm gone? I need to see him with my own eyes. Need to know he's okay." Tears sprang to the corners of her eyes, but she didn't care. Tucker had been hurt because of her, and she needed to make sure he was all right.

IRRITATION CLAWED at the back of Tucker's throat. The florescent lights in the partitioned off section of the emergency room burned his eyes just as bad as the harsh chemicals in whatever they used to clean this place.

He didn't want to be here. Hell, he didn't *need* to be here. A hit to the head wasn't enough to put him in a damn hospital bed.

But when Cruz had come across him laid out on the street,

he'd insisted on calling a medic who'd insisted on bringing him to the emergency room.

Now he needed the doctor to come back with the results of his CT so he could find out everything was all right and get the hell out of there.

Hurried footsteps skittering down the hall had him straightening on the inclined bed. Someone moving that fast couldn't be a good thing. Which meant his test results had just fallen low on the priority list for the understaffed county hospital.

A stab of guilt pierced him as the steps grew closer and the white curtain that boxed him into his makeshift room whipped open.

Elizabeth flew inside, her blond hair hanging loose and a little disheveled, over her shoulders. She'd draped her purse across her body, and fear shone bright from her wide eyes. "Tucker! Oh my God."

Shock stole any response he could come up with.

She crossed the room and threw her arms around his neck. Her body pressed against his, leaning him back against the mattress.

His arms wrapped around her on instinct. Pain spiked in his head and his stomach revolted from the sudden motion. But the feeling of Elizabeth in his arms made every ache worth it. He inhaled, taking in the smell of her coconut shampoo. A small groan escaped his lips.

Elizabeth jolted upright and wiped at the moisture clinging to her cheeks. "I'm sorry. Did I hurt you? I was just so scared and seeing you sitting up and not hurt made me so happy. If something would have happened to you because of me..." She pressed a hand to her lips.

He forced a smile, not wanting her to feel badly for her display of affection. Hell, he'd suffer far worse for her to do the exact same thing just one more time. "As you can see, I'm fine.

You didn't need to come all the way here. Honestly, they didn't even need to bring me to the damn hospital."

Chet stomped through the door and snorted. "Don't let him fool you. Cruz told us you blacked out. That's not fine. And yes, you need to be here. Stop complaining."

"Great," Tucker said, relaxing back against the bed. "Is there anyone who doesn't know I was blindsided?"

The pity on Elizabeth's face worked his jaw back and forth.

"All Cruz said was you blacked out after being attacked near your truck. Nothing more," Chet said. "And Mia knows, but that's it."

Tucker rolled his eyes then winced, although he didn't even know why he was annoyed. Of course Chet would tell Mia. If he lived with the woman he loved, he'd tell her every damn thing that happened throughout his day.

Chet held up a hand. "I had to tell her. She's sitting with Audrey while she naps. I didn't think Elizabeth should come alone."

Appreciation stung his eyes. "Thanks, man."

"Tell us what happened." Elizabeth sat on the edge of his bed and clutched her hands in her lap as if not sure where to place them. "I mean, I was just there. Was someone waiting for you?"

He pinched the bridge of his nose, not wanting to relive his failure. "I was walking to my truck after watching you drive away. I reached for my door handle then something hit me hard on the back of the head." His fingers drifted to the lump on center of his scalp, and he winced.

"That's horrible," Elizabeth said, her hand sliding over to rest on his.

Taking a chance, he flipped up his palm and folded his fingers over hers.

"Is this attack related to Elizabeth?" Chet asked, folding his arms over his broad chest.

He nodded, the motion sending shocks of agony through his body and glanced at Elizabeth. "He told me you were his, and if I didn't leave you alone, the next time he came for me he'd kill me."

Elizabeth's eyes filled with tears, and she squeezed his hand.

A host of emotions pressed against his chest. Her skin was so soft, so smooth. He'd gladly accept a dozen blows to the head if this was his reward.

"Did you notice anything that could be used to identify him?" Chet's instinct to snap into cop mode brought Tucker back into focus.

"No." Defeat crushed his windpipe, making it hard to speak. "He came out of nowhere. The initial blow took me completely by surprise, and he stayed at my back. The knife he held to my spine kept me from sneaking a peek, then the blow to my temple knocked me out. Guy knew what he was doing. Knew exactly where to strike to make sure I couldn't go after him."

Elizabeth's face went white. "You didn't mention he had a knife. He could have killed you right then."

He wanted to argue, to insist he could have handled the situation if it had escalated, but the fact he was sitting on a bed in the emergency room told a different story.

The curtains rustled and a nurse in dark blue scrubs with a kind face and black-framed glasses stepped in. "Sorry to interrupt, but you're good to go. Just try to relax the next few days. Headaches, nausea, and even some dizziness are all normal with head injuries. Even minor ones. But if things get worse— blurred vision, passing out, inability to function—come back and see us immediately."

"Okay," he said, glad to finally get the go-ahead to leave.

"Also, wouldn't be the worst idea not to be alone tonight." She handed him some paperwork then smiled at Elizabeth. "Concussions can be tricky. Especially the first night afterward. Another set of eyes keeping watch is always a good thing."

Elizabeth's face burned red, and she slipped her hand away from his.

He fought against the stab of disappointment at her retreat. "Thanks."

Once she was gone, he slowly swung his legs over the side of the bed. His brain rattled in his skull, and he blinked to stop the room from spinning. "Let's get out of here."

"I'll drive us all to your truck, then Elizabeth can drive you back to the retreat. That way you don't have to leave your vehicle in town."

"Thanks, but I can drive my own truck when we get there."

Elizabeth stood with both hands anchored on her hips. "Don't think so. I get to be your chauffeur this time, and don't even think about fighting me on this. If I can wear Audrey down, I can wear you down."

Grinning, he bit back any more arguments. His head was killing him, his stomach roiled with every movement, but Elizabeth had come to his side when he'd been injured. That was enough to lift his spirits. He'd focus on his injury and the man who'd put him in the hospital later. For once, he just wanted to lose himself in the good and enjoy the company of the beautiful woman about to drive him home.

11

After failing to convince Tucker to let her take him home, Elizabeth stayed close to his side as he settled into a rocking chair on the small patio in front of the kennel. She'd checked with Mia, who'd assured her Audrey was still sleeping, and wanted to get Tucker situated before heading back inside. He might not have taken what the nurse had to say seriously, but she had. He needed someone to keep an eye on him for the next twenty-four hours.

And even if she'd been embarrassed that her display of affection caused the older woman to make assumptions about their relationship, she had no qualms being the one to make sure Tucker was okay. Especially since she was partially responsible for his injuries.

"Is there anything I can get you?"

"You can stop hovering," he snapped then winced and drifted his hand over Otto's head, who laid beside him on the stamped concrete. "Sorry."

She lifted a shoulder and pushed her hair behind her ear. "No need to apologize. I don't like being hovered over either but that hasn't stopped everyone from showing up to help the last couple days. It feels nice to be the one doing the looking after for once."

The side of his mouth hitched up, but he kept his gaze fixed on the lake. "Never thought of it like that."

"It's always easier to look at things from our own points of view." A subtle breeze rippled over the water and danced up her arms. The stirring of air beat back the oppressive heat of the day.

She studied the tiny waves as they lapped onto the pebbled shore. Maybe she could bring Audrey here when she woke. Pretend she was letting her search for pretty stones instead of staying close to Tucker in case something happened. He might see right through her plan, but her gut told her he'd let her keep up the pretense.

Tucker grunted. "For most people that's true. But not you. You could always see to the core of a problem from everyone's perspective. That's why you were so damn good at your job."

His praise warmed her cheeks, but a punch of sadness lingered inside her. As much as she liked teaching, she'd loved being a profiler. "I miss it."

She hadn't meant to say the words. Not to Tucker, who understood exactly why she'd quit. The thought brought an onslaught of painful memories to the surface, and she sank onto the wooden rocking chair beside him. "I miss *him*."

The admission sucked the air from her body, and she collapsed against the back of her seat. She seldom spoke of Gary, at least not in an I-miss-the-man-I-loved type of way. Her conversations about Gary were centered around silly stories and his favorite flavors of ice cream. Things that amused Audrey, and that gave her a little bit of insight into who her father had been.

But it never went beyond that. Wasting time thinking about what her life could have been and missing the person who would have made them a completed family was too painful.

Not only because it was a reminder of everything Audrey would never have, but it also held up a mirror she was forced to look at. And when she faced that mirror, nothing but guilt and anger stared back at her.

Because as much as she hated to admit it, she was fine without him, which made her a heartless monster.

"I miss him, too." Tucker let out a long sigh. "He would have been so damn proud of you and that little girl you've raised. Would have been the best dad."

"I hate she never got to meet him." She slowly rocked the chair back and forth and watched a hawk swoop down from one of the trees bordering the lake. "I try to tell Audrey as much as I can, but I hate to admit there's so much I don't know."

"I have a lot of stories," he said, voice tight. "Haven't thought about them in a long time. Every time I try, I just think about all the ways I let him down. And now, I'm letting you down. He'd kick my ass if he were here."

She frowned. "How in the world have you let me down? You've stuck to my side since the shooting. Helped find my daughter and me a safe place to stay. You've been wonderful."

His jaw dropped at her heartfelt confession, and she let her gaze fall to her lap.

He cleared his throat. "I let my guard down. That guy should have never been able to sneak up on me like that. I should have seen him or grabbed him or something to put a stop to this whole thing. Gary wouldn't have let that happen. He would have been alert. Caught this sonofabitch so he couldn't even think about hurting you or Audrey."

"There's nothing you've done that he would have done any differently. None of this is your fault. If anyone here's to blame, it's me. You were at the police station because of me. You're involved in this whole mess because of me."

He turned and faced her, disbelief shining bright in his blue eyes. "If you meant what you said earlier about me not being responsible for Gary's death—that it was his decision to run into that building after me and Otto, then you have to know nothing that has happened is your fault. I was hurt because someone out there doesn't want me near you—has staked some sick claim over you. You didn't ask for any of this."

"But you were hurt because of me. Because of your relationship to me." Shock stole her voice as thoughts clicked into place. He opened his mouth to speak, but she waved her hands through the air and shushed him. "Wait a second. What if the same thing happened to Paul?"

Tucker's eyebrows snapped low. "What do you mean?"

"The police assumed he was the target because of his criminal activity, but what if he was the target for another reason? What if someone wanted to erase him from the equation, take out the man who constantly hounded me for a date?"

Tucker ran his hand over Otto's head as if the feel of his dog helped him think. "Makes sense. Especially given the threat that was issued to me. I'm new to this equation, which means this person has kept an eye on you enough to know I've been around a lot and he doesn't like it. How long had Paul pestered you to go out with him?"

Realization shivered down her spine. "Close to a year. Do you think someone has been obsessed with me all that time?"

"I don't know, but the bigger question is who all knew your co-worker had a thing for you?"

She squeezed her eyes closed for a beat, understanding what she'd have to do. She'd hoped that whoever they sought was capable of gaining information about her and her life by loitering on the periphery of her social circle. Hell, even by watching from afar, which was creepy as hell. But as time went by, only one thing was certain. Whoever thought she belonged to him—thought that she and Audrey were a part of his family —was someone who was privy to more than just the superficial areas of her life.

Now, she just needed to pinpoint who.

AN HOUR LATER, the sound of giggling drew Tucker's attention away from the list of names he was studying. He had no doubt Elizabeth had concocted some kind of excuse to get Audrey down to the kennel. But he didn't mind one bit. If he could hear that giggle every day for the rest of his life, he'd die a happy man.

As it was, Audrey's excitement over wading ankle-deep in the cool lake with his friend Zoe and picking out pebbles meant he and Elizabeth could give a little more thought over the question of who was responsible for tormenting them.

"Don't go any further," Elizabeth called from her spot beside him and Cruz on the patio.

Not even fifteen feet separated mother from daughter, but he understood her trepidation. "Otto's right there. He won't let her wander. And neither will Zoe."

Zoe Peyton, Cruz's girlfriend and the retreat's yoga instructor, turned from her spot behind Audrey and waved. "I got her." She'd accompanied him to the kennel with their puppy, Bacchus. The bundle of wrinkles didn't like the water as much as Otto and stayed glued to the shoreline with her tail wagging and adorable face fixed on Audrey.

"Zoe heard about all the fun Mia had with Audrey earlier and had to stop by," Cruz said with a small snort. "Your daughter has a mass of swooning fans here, ready and willing to do whatever she wants."

Elizabeth rolled her eyes. "Great. Just what she needs." Her gaze darted from Audrey's sun-kissed face and high ponytail to the pup watching her every move.

Tucker could sense her tension. "I trained Bacchus myself. She's a good girl and wouldn't hurt a flea."

She flashed a tight smile. "She looks intimidating."

Cruz laughed. "Sure, until she licks you to death or runs and hides from the vacuum. I've never met a bigger scaredy cat in my life."

Elizabeth's gaze lingered a second longer before returning her focus to the list she'd just completed. "I hate this."

"What?" Tucker and Cruz asked in unison.

"This," she said, flicking her wrist toward the list. "Writing down the name of any man I can think of. Anyone I see regularly or sticks out in my mind. Friends. Cashiers. My neighbors. It feels so invasive. Like I don't trust anyone. I've never been on this side of things before. It's much harder than I anticipated."

"Do you trust every man on that list? Is there anyone on there that you'd trust with your life? With Audrey's?" Cruz asked, crossing his arms over his chest.

"No." She cringed, as if she didn't like the answer.

But this was a time when brutal honesty was necessary. No matter what kind of lens it forced over the people in Elizabeth's life.

"You didn't list your coworkers. The three men we ate breakfast with," Tucker said.

Frowning, the energy around her shifted. "But they ran outside the building with the rest of the faculty right before the shooting took place. They couldn't have been responsible."

"Did you see them there?" Cruz asked.

She narrowed her eyes, thinking. "I saw Sebastian right before the fire alarm went off. He was on his way to the staff meeting. Ed and Scott were probably already in the room."

"What about outside?" Tucker asked. "When the shooting occurred."

"I...I don't think so. But it all happened so fast, and I was panicked. Not to mention Paul was driving me crazy and I was trying to keep from snapping at him. Then the gun went off and everyone fell to the ground. I guess I didn't get a good look at every face there. I can't say for certain Scott, Ed, and Sebastian were outside at that moment."

Tucker shared a quick look with Cruz before asking his next question. "If we go with the theory that Paul was targeted based on his relationship with you, someone had to have known he was there. The attack was planned. Besides the faculty members, who would have known both you and Paul would be on campus?"

She chewed her bottom lip. "Either the staff or anyone close to the staff. Courtney, my nanny, would have known because I needed a sitter for the meeting. Same would be true for anyone else in the department. Spouses, caregivers, children....hell, maybe even close friends. That's an awfully large net to cast considering we can't be sure who would be aware of everyone's schedules."

"But we can talk to the staff," Cruz cut in. "Ask them for lists of people who they'd spoken with about the faculty meeting. Add to that we are looking for someone who's a damn good shot. Ballistic reports came back. Looks like the bullet was from a McMillon Tac."

Tucker let out a long whistle. "Damn. Guy could be ex-military then."

Frowning, Cruz nodded. "My thoughts exactly."

Elizabeth plucked the top sheet of paper from the pile. "We can't bet on that, but if we work with that angle, it will eliminate a lot of potential suspects."

"Do you know of anyone on that list that served?" Cruz asked.

She shook her head. "I'm not very close with any of them. I don't have the time. Between work and Audrey, socializing and making friends falls pretty far on my list of priorities. I speak with Ed the most because we both lost a spouse and have a child. We relate to each other. Sebastian, he's a nice guy who's always clowning around. Tries to coax me out of my office but never in a creepy way. We've never gone further than surface level friendship. And Scott, we've barely said more than a handful of words to one another. But if we're looking for a military man, it won't be hard to find out if any of them served."

"What about your nanny?" Tucker hated asking the question, especially with the shocked look that darkened her face.

She reared back her head as if the question physically assaulted her. "What about her?"

He took his time with his answer, not wanting to offend. "You mentioned not having time for friends, but I assume you two are together a lot."

Clenching her jaw, she nodded. "What's your point?"

"She's recently married, correct?"

Again, she nodded.

"Courtney would know your schedule better than anyone, and I'd assume her husband would know where she is. Which would mean he'd have knowledge of your whereabouts. Maybe not specific details, but he could put two and two together if he wanted. Plus the photo that was put on your phone's home screen is from their wedding. Could mean something."

The shifting of Elizabeth's eyes and the way she moved her lips in a subtle way back and forth told him that something had dawned on her that made her uncomfortable. "What is it?"

She swallowed hard, her wide-eyed stare meeting his. "Courtney's husband, Caleb, served in the Army for four years. He was a sniper. He could have made the shot that killed Paul from a mile away."

12

Elizabeth's stomach rolled, but she couldn't be sure if it was due to the conversation she'd had with Tucker and Cruz thirty minutes before, or the way Audrey ran with the therapy dogs. Her daughter bounced around the wide, fenced-in enclosure beside the kennel grinning from ear-to-ear as she threw tennis balls and showered love on each canine she encountered.

Tucker was inside, going over the benefits of using dogs for therapy with one of the new guests at the retreat. She kept forgetting he had a job to do. He'd devoted himself so completely to helping her and Audrey that the everyday aspects of his life slipped through the cracks of her awareness.

Zoe sat beside her at a picnic table in the middle of the play area. Her auburn locks were tied high on her head in a messy bun, and picture-perfect yoga clothes showed off her long, toned frame. "Your daughter is adorable. Thank you for letting me spend time with you two."

"She loves being spoiled by so many people. We really appreciate everyone's generosity." Her eyes drifted to the window that looked into the kennel.

Zoe bumped her with her shoulder. "We've all enjoyed having you both around. Especially Tucker."

Words escaped her, so she sat in the quiet, absorbing the warmth of the sun on her skin as she watched her daughter having fun, the peaks of the mountains rising above the tree line in the distance. She wished she could escape all the questions mounting higher in her mind and just pretend it was an ordinary day in a beautiful setting. But that wasn't possible.

A few moments passed before Zoe asked, "How are you holding up?"

She tossed the question around in her head before answering with a small shrug. "I'm scared but trying not to think too much about what's happening so Audrey doesn't sense something's wrong. At the same time, none of this seems real. Like this couldn't be happening to me. I mean, I worked countless cases where I helped chase down some of the worst criminals imaginable. I never thought one of those criminals would target me and my daughter."

"I understand." Zoe's voice turned soft and distant.

Elizabeth stared at her with narrowed eyes. "You do?" She hated the note of skepticism in her tone, but how could anyone understand what she was going through?

A haunted expression took over the delicate features of Zoe's face. "Not that long ago, someone targeted me."

Shame slammed against her. "I'm so sorry. What happened?"

Zoe sighed and scrunched up her nose. "Short version, someone created a delusional fantasy. It almost cost me my life."

"That's horrible," Elizabeth said, gripping Zoe's hand. "I'm so glad you're okay."

A small smile lifted Zoe's lips. "Me, too. As tough as it was to get through, I came out the other end with a better grasp of past traumas and Cruz. Not to mention this bundle of wrinkles." She leaned over and pressed a kiss to the well-behaved dog glued to her side.

The comment piqued Elizabeth's curiosity and she couldn't help wanting to find out more. "You and Cruz weren't an item before?" She hadn't spent much time around Cruz and Zoe, but the couple appeared so in synch she'd assumed they'd been together forever.

Zoe shook her head. "We were friends for years. Neither of us were willing to admit there were feelings there, especially when we were both battling our own demons. What we didn't realize was that we're stronger together than we could ever be apart."

The glow that erupted from Zoe as she talked had pangs of jealousy wiggling like nasty tentacles through Elizabeth. The description of their former relationship made her think of Tucker. They were friends...sort of. They both had trauma from the past impacting their lives, but it was a shared demon that tormented them.

"What's that look about?" Zoe asked.

Schooling her features, Elizabeth slipped her hand from Zoe's and refocused on Audrey and the yard of tail-wagging dogs. "I don't know what you mean."

"Yes, you do, but you don't need to tell me. We barely know each other. Just remember, almost everyone here has gone through some bad things and survived. We're all here for you. No matter if you want to talk or just sit around and watch your child play."

Appreciation pressed against her chest. She didn't have a lot of close friends she could vent to. No one she could just unload her troubles and talk through her issues with. Well, no one besides Courtney, who wasn't as much a friend as an employee and now her husband was on the suspect list. Geez, her life was so messed up it made her want to tear out her hair.

Making sure Audrey was out of earshot, she summoned up

more strength than it should take to spill her guts and decided to trust the woman beside her. "Your story with Cruz sounds similar, but Tucker and I are a lot more complicated."

"Everyone thinks their story is more complicated than everyone else's." Zoe held up her palms. "I don't say that to be judgmental. Just stating the obvious."

"Who else do you know whose new husband and father of her child was killed because his best friend charged into a building to save his dog?" Her voice cracked and she held in the part she'd never dared say out loud—that constant guilt gnawed at her gut because of the tiny embers of attraction she'd always buried for Tucker.

Attraction that was annoyingly close to the surface after spending so much time with him this week.

Sympathy swam in Zoe's green eyes. "No one else I'm aware of. But my story isn't much prettier. Anytime you want to hear it, all you've got to do is ask. Until then, just know I'm always looking for new friends."

"Friends are something I need more of in my life."

"Good. Then I can use you as a guinea pig for my classes. How do you feel about yoga?"

She lifted one shoulder, not wanting to admit she'd had even less time for working out than she did for friends. "I'm more of a take a hike kind of girl but I'm willing to try anything."

"I have a Mommy and Me class I teach at my studio in town. You should bring Audrey tomorrow. Tucker, too. He's actually pretty good."

She couldn't stop her jaw from dropping, or the heat from rushing up the back of her neck at the thought of watching Tucker bend and twist in intricate poses.

"Yep," Zoe said with a chuckle. "He looks pretty good while doing it."

Elizabeth grinned. "Tucker doesn't seem like the yoga type."

"He's full of surprises, and I bet if you let him show you, you'd be pretty impressed with all of them."

Elizabeth had a feeling Zoe was right, but she wasn't sure if she could handle any more surprises from Tucker. Her walls had already started to crumble, and it wouldn't take much to destroy her all over again.

She'd barely been able to walk away from Tucker the first time his actions had broken her heart. If it happened again, she didn't know if she'd survive.

CANINE THERAPY WAS ALWAYS a big draw at the retreat, something that delighted Tucker. Most of the guests weren't comfortable diving right into the different types of rehabilitation that were provided and often opted to start with physical activities or the dogs.

But today, he just wanted to be done with work so he could focus on Elizabeth. Not to mention he felt like shit after his brush with her stalker.

The sound of her laughter leaked through the open window. He watched her for a second, smile wide and focus on Zoe. Damn, he loved his friends. Zoe might have claimed to want to spend time with Audrey, but all his closest pals had rallied together to make sure the mother-daughter duo were never alone. Even for the brief moments he was mere feet away on the other side of the wall. He'd hit the jackpot when he'd come home to Pine Valley. He had everything he needed. Too bad the one thing he'd do anything to have was just beyond his reach.

Or was it?

A few tender moments had passed between him and Elizabeth since he'd stumbled upon her after the shooting. Then there was the incident at the hospital. Her flying to his side then throwing herself into his arms had to mean something.

But if it didn't, or those moments had meant more to him than her, he could put the whole delicate balance they'd found in jeopardy. Now that he'd spent time with Audrey, he couldn't imagine walking away and never seeing her again. Never sharing stories about her father with her. One wrong move with Elizabeth would put an end to any further discussion of him seeing Audrey after the dust settled.

A thought for another day. Because today, the dust was anything but settled and his only concern should be keeping Elizabeth and her daughter safe.

"Come on, Otto," he said, snapping his fingers.

Otto raced over and zipped through the door to the play area as soon as Tucker opened it.

Audrey squealed in delight and made a beeline for Otto.

Elizabeth sought him out with concern in her hazel eyes. "How are you holding up?"

He shrugged, not ready to tell her how bad his head hurt, then settled beside her on the picnic table. He leaned forward, resting his forearms on his knees, and kept his attention on Otto as the dog wagged his tail and licked Audrey's cheek. "I think he has a new best friend."

"Never. You'll always be his favorite," Zoe said, hopping to her feet. Bacchus stood beside her, head cocked to the side as if understanding every word she'd said. "I have to take off, but I told Elizabeth she should come to my Mommy and Me class tomorrow. Audrey might like it."

He didn't relish the idea of Elizabeth venturing off the property alone, but he held his tongue. It wasn't up to him to give his opinions on her actions. She was a smart woman who could make her own choices. "Didn't realize you were into yoga."

"I could say the same about you." She bumped her thigh against his and grinned.

"I'm all for anything that puts me in a good head space."

"Which is why we love him around here. Hopefully I'll see you guys tomorrow." Zoe waved then shouted a goodbye to Audrey before she let herself and her sidekick out through the gate.

Tucker waited until Zoe started up the hill before he asked, "You really thinking about going?"

"Only if you come with me." She nibbled her bottom lip, as if her admission made her nervous.

The thought of moving in any of the poses Zoe tossed out made his stomach roll, but he'd never admit it. "If you want me there, I'm there."

She dropped her gaze to her hands clutched in her lap. "Then let's do it. As long as you're feeling all right."

"I should be fine. I asked Izzy who works the front desk to cover for me here. There aren't any other guests who need my attention, and she's great with the dogs. She'll make sure they're taken care of for the night."

Elizabeth tilted her head to the side. "Will she sleep here? Your house isn't on the property, and I never thought about what you do with the dogs overnight. Seems sad to think of them all alone at night."

"Never thought you'd be worried about my dogs," he teased.

"Oh, shush." She playfully slapped at his chest.

Taking a chance, he captured her hand before she could pull away and kept it pinned to him. "I like your concern. For me and the dogs."

She blushed but didn't try to escape his grasp.

He lowered their joined hands onto the bench seat between them. "To answer your question, no one sleeps here with the dogs. Brooke's cabin is close. She or Lincoln will check on them before they turn in for the night. I have cameras all over the place inside. I can monitor what's going on from my house, and the night staff up at the lodge have screens in the employee lounge to keep an eye on things as well. If anything is needed, someone will be there quick to help."

Otto bounded over and plopped on the ground by Elizabeth's feet. He breathed heavily, his mouth open as if smiling while he watched the other dogs continue to play with the little girl.

Elizabeth reached down to pat the top of his head, and Tucker couldn't help but smile.

Maybe, after all this time, he might have a chance to get everything he ever wanted after all.

13

A yawn ripped through Elizabeth as she pushed stray peas around her dinner plate. The dining room was mostly empty, dirty dishes left on the square tables scattered around the room. Between keeping up with Audrey's excitement all day, mentally wading through all the information she had on the men she'd passed along to Cruz and trying to sort through her feelings for Tucker, she was exhausted.

"What's after dinner, Mommy?" Audrey bounced up and down on her bottom and shoveled mashed potatoes into her mouth. "More swimming?"

Tucker groaned and gave an exaggerated eye roll. "Don't you ever get tired?"

Audrey grinned. "Nope."

"Welcome to my life." Elizabeth stared out the large window at the darkening sky. The sun had disappeared behind the mountaintops, but the lingering glow left a swirl of deep orange and purple hovering above the tree-tipped peaks. She'd give her right arm to sit on the deck and enjoy the view with a giant glass of wine.

Instead, she sipped her water and aimed her smile at

Audrey. She braced herself for the argument she was sure would come. "Sweetheart, it's getting close to bedtime, and we've had a super busy day. We need to head back to our room when we're done eating." She didn't mention her desperate desire to dive into the files waiting for her. If she was going to help find the man after her, she needed to get into his head.

"But we still haven't given Otto a walk." Audrey smothered the words in a pathetic whine.

Elizabeth struggled to reign in her impatience. She'd given her daughter everything she wanted the last two days, showering her with more attention than normal. But now wasn't the time to let Audrey pick yet another activity.

"It's too late to take Otto for a walk," Tucker said, rescuing her from saying something she'd regret. "The sun's going down, and he needs to go to bed soon."

Audrey scrunched her nose. "Where is his bed?"

Amusement lifted one side of Tucker's mouth. "His bed is at my house."

She frowned. "But don't you live here?"

"Nope. My house is about ten minutes up the mountain."

Her face fell. "When you take Otto to bed, you'll leave me?"

A mixture of sadness and anxiety pressed down on Elizabeth's chest. She wanted to swoop in and wipe the pain off her daughter's face, but she couldn't. Couldn't erase the hurt now at the thought of Tucker walking out of her life, and she couldn't ease it all the times Audrey watched other little girls walk hand in hand with their daddies.

Tucker set his fork down and pivoted toward Audrey. "When I take Otto home, I'll leave the retreat. Which is just the place where I work. But I'll never leave you. Not if you don't want me to."

Audrey frowned. "But you won't be here when I go to sleep?"

Elizabeth sucked in a breath, waiting for Audrey's meltdown, and brokenhearted to see her daughter so distraught over Tucker not being around.

He turned to meet her eye, as if asking for permission to continue his conversation in his way, and she gave a subtle nod. This was a foreign situation for her, and she wasn't sure which step would fall on a land mine and which would placate Audrey. If he was willing to figure it out, she'd give him a chance, and dammit it if his effort didn't thaw her resistance toward him even more.

"What if Otto and I walk you and your mom back to your room? Maybe we can hang out until you're asleep."

Excitement lit Audrey's eyes. "Can he, Mommy?"

Her core tightened. They'd spent countless hours together the last few days, but this would be different. This would be a snapshot of what their life could be, and she wasn't sure if she could handle witnessing it. If she kept falling for this man, she'd surely be crushed sooner or later.

"Mommy?" Audrey asked again.

"Sure," she said, quieting the butterflies in her stomach before glancing up at Tucker. "If we're all finished eating, we can head back there now. I want to get some work done. If you're there, you can look through the files with me and give me your input."

"Sounds good. Let me clear the plates." Tucker stood and gathered their dirty dishes then ferried them to the kitchen, returning minutes later with a slow smile. "Ready?"

Oh boy, was she. At least she thought she was. When all this was over, she really needed to examine where her head and heart were then have a conversation with Tucker. Surrendering to her emotions now wasn't a smart decision. She couldn't trust herself, and she liked the idea of Tucker being around too much to risk their friendship. Especially when Gary's ghost lingered between them.

Everything else around her disappeared in a haze of nerves

as she walked with Audrey's hand in hers, Tucker on her daughter's other side, down the hall and back to their temporary room. Otto trotted in front of them as if he knew the way. She unlocked the door just as her phone vibrated in the front pocket of her shorts.

She maneuvered across the threshold, allowing space for Tucker and Audrey to enter, before plucking out her phone and checking the number. "This is Sebastian," she said. "I'll just be a minute."

Tucker closed and locked the door then crouched low, saying something she couldn't hear that made Audrey giggle.

Accepting the call, she took a seat at the table where she could keep an eye on the room. "Hi, Sebastian."

"Hey. Just checking in. How are you holding up?" Cheerfulness that she didn't quite believe lifted his words.

She shrugged, even though he couldn't see her. "I'm okay."

"Want pizza? I could grab some and head over for a few minutes. I need to get out of my house. I'll get Fisher's. Audrey's favorite, right?"

She smiled and relaxed against the back of her chair. Earlier in the day she'd fretted about not having any friends. Sometimes she forgot how sweet her coworkers were. Spending time one on one with her colleagues didn't happen often. She needed to change that. "That's a nice offer, but Audrey and I left town for a couple days."

He sighed. "Seems like everyone had the same idea. Maybe that's what I should do. My mind keeps going to these dark places. I'm jumpy and scared. A few days away might be good for me."

Bemused, she watched Audrey rifle through her bag and pull out her favorite bedtime book then lead Tucker to the sofa. He sat and pulled her onto his lap and she nearly swooned.

"Elizabeth?" Sebastian asked. "You still there?"

"Sorry, I had to help Audrey and got distracted." The lie

tasted bitter on her tongue, but she couldn't confess where her mind had really been. "I'm sorry you're having a rough time. Living through such a traumatic experience can have lasting effects. Maybe try Ed."

"I already did. He's MIA."

Straightening, she frowned. "What do you mean?"

"I've tried calling him all day. Even stopped by his place. He's gone and won't answer his phone. He was acting pretty twitchy yesterday, and we just assumed it was because of the shooting and the killer still being out there, but I don't know... I'm worried about him. He's shut him and Oliver away. It's not like him."

As a single parent herself, she understood the hassle of taking a nine-month-old child anywhere alone. Especially spur of the moment. The fact Ed would just take off with the baby didn't sit well with her. "You guys are pretty close. Is there anyone you could contact to find out where he went?"

"The only people we have in common are from the college. My guess, he needed time away. Like we all do. I just wish he'd have opened up a little. At a time like this, we should be there for each other."

Her gaze traveled back to Tucker, quietly reading to a sleepy Audrey. He'd been there for her when she'd needed him most. What about everyone else? She wished she could offer Sebastian more insight, but he hadn't been cleared from her list of suspects. Although the answer to just one little question could ease her mind a lot.

"Do you know if Ed served in the military?"

Sebastian chuckled. "That's random, but actually, yeah. We've talked about it a few times. We both served. I left the Army about three years ago, and Ed's time was up about two years ago. Right before you started at the college."

And just like that, two more names went to the top of her list.

BY THE TIME Tucker read the last word in the silly, rhyming book, Audrey's head fell on his shoulder and her breaths evened out. His heart expanded in his chest. He didn't want this moment to end—didn't want to lay this little girl down and walk away.

Elizabeth carried over a bottle of beer and handed it to him before sitting on the opposite end of the couch. "Is this okay for you to have with the blow to your head earlier?"

"I'll take my chances. Thanks." He carefully placed the book on the coffee table then took a sip of his beer. "How does she fall asleep so fast? I swear, I lay in bed for hours before I drift off."

"You probably don't play as hard as she does. Between running with the dogs, collecting pebbles, swimming, and enjoying all the attention heaped upon her, she barely stops moving for a second when she's awake." She lifted the bottle to her lips and took a sip before placing it on the coffee table. "Do you want me to put her in bed?"

The suggestion had him tightening his hold on her. "Nah. Not yet."

"While you were reading, I talked to Sebastian and got some interesting information."

He quirked up an eyebrow. "What's that?"

She ran her hand through her long strands, tossing her hair in an exaggerated part over the side of her head. "Sebastian said Ed's nowhere to be found. That he was shook up and now he's just gone."

Tucker bounced the information around his head. "I'm sure everyone who was there is shaken up. Hell, it'd be tough not to be. Him being unreachable isn't exactly groundbreaking news, although could be a red flag."

She nodded as though in agreement. "I took the opportunity to ask if either had been in the military. Both served."

He whistled low, not wanting to wake Audrey still snuggled against him. "That makes three men who know you and your routine that all have ties to the military. We need to let Cruz and Lincoln know. How well do you know these men?"

She turned to the window and let her gaze rest there for a beat. "Caleb is around with Courtney a lot. I trust him, or at least I did. He spends time with Audrey, is at the house from time to time. I wouldn't say I know him well. He's my employee's husband. Mainly I trust her, and I trust her judgement."

Her nanny would be the person who'd be the most aware of her schedule. She was with Audrey at the time of the shooting, and no way she was the person who'd attacked him on the street, but could she play a role? Even if she wasn't aware? "Has she ever confided anything about him? Does he have a temper? Want a family? Jealousy an issue?"

"No, nothing. They're newlyweds. Beyond the typical annoyance about dirty socks left on the floor, she's never said a negative thing about him."

"I never understood why women get so mad about that. I mean, they're just socks."

She scrunched her nose. "*Dirty* socks that need placed in the hamper."

He took another drink of his cold beer, loving the new and easy comradery they'd developed in such a short span of time. "Agree to disagree. But back to the other two men. Either ever give you bad vibes?"

She blew out a long breath. "No, but I've never paid much attention. If I really think about it, we're looking for someone who doesn't just want me, but my family. My daughter." Her voice cracked on the last word.

Needing to comfort her, he set his drink on the end table and reached across the middle cushion to find her hand.

"Ed," she said, eyes wide and unblinking. "He's the one who lost a wife. And Sebastian mentioned he'd left the military right before I started at the college. We've discussed being single parents and how tough it can be. How much easier life could be with a partner. You don't think he took that to mean *I* should be his partner, do you?"

Her confession sat like lead in his gut. She didn't have a partner because that fateful night, the bust she'd assisted them on took a tragic turn. She'd lost her new partner in life, and he'd lost his best friend. "If he took that leap, it's not because of anything you said when confiding in a friend."

She swished her lips to the side. "It's so much harder on this side of it. Harder to see the truth about the people in my life, harder to convince myself about things that are normally so logical. I'm glad you're here with me. I don't think I could go through this alone."

"You could do anything you want, however you want. But I'm sorry you don't have a partner to help with Audrey and all the demands of life. I'm sorry that was taken from you."

She traced her thumbnail over his knuckle and averted her gaze. "I would have loved to have Gary by my side during my pregnancy and the birth of our daughter. To help me with midnight feedings and meltdowns. But he was never my partner. Not in the way people assume."

Her words shocked him. "I don't understand what you mean."

"Mommy?" Audrey whimpered and thrashed in his arms.

Elizabeth jerked her hand from his and stood. "I'm right here, baby. Let's get you into bed."

She scooped the little bundle from his lap and an emptiness nearly swallowed him whole.

"Sorry. When she wakes like this, it's tough to get her back down. This might take a while."

Audrey buried her head in Elizabeth's chest. "I want Otto,"

she cried. "I don't want to go to bed. Tucker." She reached out a hand to him, and his heart fell to the floor.

Otto sprung to his feet, sensing the tension in the air, and ran to Elizabeth's side.

"Do you want help?" He jumped up, wanting to do something but having no idea what.

"Honestly, I just need to lay her down and rub her back or she'll never get settled."

"But Otto." Tears leaked from Audrey's eyes in the most pathetic display of sadness Tucker had ever seen.

"Shh, honey. You have to go back to sleep." Elizabeth kissed her cheek and carried her to the bed, laying her gently on the mattress.

Otto leapt onto the bed beside her.

"Good boy," Audrey said, wrapping an arm over the black fur and turning on her side. Her cries stopped. Her breathing evened out.

Elizabeth fisted her hands on her hips and stared down at them for a second before swinging his way. "Well, not sure what to do now."

He watched Audrey's little chest rise and fall and the way Otto's eyes drifted shut. The twosome didn't appear as though they'd tolerate being separated. "Doesn't look like there's much you can do. If you're okay with Otto staying, I can leave him here."

Bending down, she brushed a stray hair off Audrey's forehead then ran her hand over Otto's head. "I don't think I have a choice."

He hesitated for a second, lost in the moment and wishing he could ask Elizabeth to pick up where she'd left off. But whatever she was about to say needed to come from her in the moment she was ready. That moment was clearly over. "I should take off. Don't want to wake her again."

"Are you sure? You don't have to." Her eyes grew round, and

he saw something deep within the specks of yellow in her irises.

As much as he wanted to stay, it wasn't a good idea. Not now. Not yet. He shoved his hands in the front pockets of his jeans and met her at the side of the bed. He stared down at Audrey and pushed aside the same strand of hair Elizabeth had moved moments before. "She's beautiful. Just like her mother." Her hazel eyes went wide, mouth open as if in surprise, and Tucker wished he could see inside her mind. "I'll be by in the morning." He pressed a kiss to Elizabeth's cheek then turned and did the hardest thing he'd ever done.

He walked away.

14

The harsh rays of the morning sun streamed into Elizabeth's eyes. She squinted and held open her arms to catch Audrey as she hurled herself from Tucker's truck. "You ready for some yoga, love bug?" She kissed her forehead and placed her on the ground.

"Why couldn't Otto come?" she asked.

Elizabeth fought not to groan. From the moment she'd woken, Audrey had been a handful—only happy when the dog was by her side. Something that would be a real pain in the ass when the time came to return home...without Otto.

Tucker rounded the hood of the vehicle and ruffled the top of Audrey's head. "Otto can't do yoga, Kiddo."

She frowned and smoothed down the puffs of hair that had come loose from her ponytail. "If he can't, I can't."

Elizabeth's groan finally slipped free. "We promised Zoe."

Audrey scrunched her nose as if deciding if that was a good enough reason to take the Mommy and Me class then her eyes widened. "I want to go there." She extended her arm and pointed toward the middle of the grassy town square.

Elizabeth turned and her jaw dropped. "What in the world?"

"I told you this weekend was a big deal around here." Tucker said. "It's always like an explosion of summer and town pride. The hay maze is new though."

"That explains the decorative flags on one corner of the street and a beachball wreath on the bakery next door," she said with a laugh. "This is insane and amazing at the same time."

When they'd driven through town the other day, a few flowers had been tied to lampposts and flags waved from storefront awnings. Business owners had drawn fun pictures on their windows ranging from mountain scenes to the hometown mascot. But nothing of this magnitude had graced the streets of Pine Valley.

"This is just the beginning," Tucker said, effortlessly taking Audrey's hand and leading her down the sidewalk. "More vendors will roll in throughout the day. Then a parade tomorrow followed by fireworks at nightfall for the grand finale. People from all over show up. I'm surprised you've never been before. Elm Ridge isn't too far. Half that town is usually here at some point over the weekend."

"Ohh! A parade!" Audrey bounced on her toes. "Can we go, Mommy?"

Elizabeth smiled down at her excited daughter. "As long as we can stop by some vendors for yummy food and swing through the hay maze."

Audrey grinned. "Deal."

The scent of fresh-baked pastries wafted from the open door of the bakery. A man in denim overalls and a red baseball hat walked outside with his toolbox in one hand and a white bag in the other. He nodded in greeting, a goofy grin on his wrinkled face. "Mornin' folks. Mrs. Crawley just pulled out a fresh sheet of coffee cake. Get it while it's hot."

Elizabeth's stomach growled.

Tucker laughed. "Morning Bob. Sounds enticing. Chet might make the best cinnamon rolls in the area, but Mrs. Crawley's coffee cake is just plain sinful. But we're headed in for a workout with Zoe."

Bob chuckled and shook his head. "Damn bad decision if you ask me. See y'all later."

Elizabeth snorted out a laugh. "I hate to say it, but I like his idea better. Yoga's not my favorite. I've never been too flexible."

"Trust me," he said, opening the door for them. "It's not my thing either. I just don't worry too much about making a fool of myself."

She chanced a peek at the toned muscles on display in his fitted black T-shirt. He claimed the baker's coffee cake was sinful, but nothing could be as delicious as the man she stepped past to enter the yoga studio. No woman alive would ever consider him foolish. Especially when bending and twisting in ways that even thinking about made her blood hum.

Audrey ran inside, her ponytail flying, and kicked off her shoes. "Up front!" She sprinted to claim her spot without waiting on anyone to follow.

She shared a hesitant look with Tucker before slipping off her sandals then placing hers and Audrey's shoes in a rack of cubbies set against the wall in the small lobby. A large window looked out on the square and showcased all the hustling townsfolk scurrying about to get everything ready for the festival. She watched for a second, pretending like she was a part of the crowd and not a guest here to escape reality for a few days.

Something about this town called to her, made her feel warm and welcomed in a way she'd never experienced. It wasn't far from her job. Would it be crazy to consider moving here? Audrey seemed to enjoy it, and friendships had formed she wanted to nurture and not run from.

Then there was Tucker. He may find her moving here suffocating, the drastic measure of a crazy woman trying to be near him. He'd probably hate that, especially after what she'd admitted the night before. The confusion in his eyes had cut her. She'd wanted to explain, to reassure him she'd loved his friend, but that their love had been too new and untested to form the type of partnership she craved.

The type of partnership Tucker could offer.

"Come on, Mommy!" Audrey yelled, waving an arm in the air. She dragged a pink yoga mat between smiling mothers and boisterous children and placed it in front of Zoe, who stood at the front of the class watching the commotion. "Tucker, I need help."

Zoe grinned, clearly amused, and offered a wave before turning her attention to a light-haired little boy who ran to her and wrapped his arms around her legs.

"We might as well get this over with," Elizabeth said, ignoring his puckered brow and narrowed eyes.

Tucker lightly gripped her arm, stopping her from walking away. "You okay? We didn't have a chance to talk about last night."

She forced a smile. "I'm fine. Just a lot on my mind. Come on, we better get our yoga mats before Audrey finds you a pink one to match hers."

"Too late." He cringed and pointed to her daughter.

She glanced over her shoulder then pressed a hand to her mouth to stifle a laugh. Audrey stood with her chin tilted up in pride, hands anchored on her tiny hips. A pink mat laid on one side of her, a purple on the other.

"Well," Elizabeth said. "At least you can choose which one you like best."

He grumbled something she couldn't understand then led the way to the front of the class. A dozen pairs of interested eyes watched him, and Elizabeth's amusement quickly turned to irritation followed by acceptance. Tucker was a piece of man candy no woman could resist. These mothers could watch all they wanted, hell, she had no claim over him.

Besides, when class was over, she'd be the only woman riding home in his truck. A tingle of excitement burst in the pit of her stomach as she settled on her mat and waited for instructions. Who knew? Maybe this class would change more than just her opinion of yoga. It just might show her a side of Tucker that she'd never be able to forget.

TUCKER WANTED to scowl after Zoe shot him a wink before starting the yoga class with gentle stretching. The pain pills he'd taken with breakfast helped the constant ache in his head. But nothing could stop the sensation of being watched from every single angle. When he'd agreed to accompany Audrey and Elizabeth to class, he'd imaged a handful of participates and tone-downed moves. Not downward facing dog and cat pose where his every move would be scrutinized.

Hell, he hated to admit it, but part of the draw was seeing Elizabeth in her yoga outfit. Now that he'd been ogled by most of the women in class, he felt like a pig for even thinking of watching her as she focused on her moves, as well as making sure Audrey understood what was happening.

"Ms. Zoe," a little boy behind him whispered. "I got a pet fish yesterday."

Zoe smiled and shifted into chair pose. "That's very exciting, Ronnie. But let's talk about that after class, okay?"

Tucker shook his head and struggled to contain his amusement. Man, kids were funny. He'd never really thought about having one of his own. Never pictured loving a woman enough to want one. He'd fallen hard for Elizabeth once and hadn't planned to do it again. But after spending time with Audrey, the idea of her going back home and his life returning to normal made his chest ache.

Not wanting to think about what the future held, he lost himself in the motion of the moves. Damn, Zoe wasn't taking it easy on these kids. Each move pulled at his muscles and tested his endurance. His shoulders burned and legs shook just a bit until he almost whimpered in relief when Zoe stood straight and pressed her palms together in prayer pose.

"Namaste," she said, dipping her head forward.

The class echoed the word back then chattering erupted as kids stormed forward to fight for Zoe's attention.

"That was fun," Audrey said. "Can we do this again?"

"Sure, honey. But before we start talking about next time, we need to clean our mats. Let's grab some sanitizing wipes, okay?"

"Can you grab one for me, munchkin?" Tucker asked.

Audrey shot him a disgruntled look.

He stuck out his tongue and she giggled as she took her mom's hand and skipped toward the dispenser set up in the corner of the room with cleaning supplies for the clients.

A hand on his bicep turned his head away from the giggling girl. He found himself staring into familiar blue eyes, though he couldn't put a name with the face.

"Hi," she said, flashing her straight, white teeth. "You probably don't remember me, but I saw you at the diner in Elm Ridge yesterday."

Recognition dawned on him. "Oh, right. The hostess. How are you?"

"Good. I'm surprised to see you here. My name's Leslie, by the way."

"Tucker." He offered a hand.

She slipped her palm in his, keeping it firmly planted for a few beats longer than necessary before pulling away. "Your first time here with your daughter?" She nodded at Audrey.

The idea that Audrey was his twisted his gut. "First time but she's not my daughter." Not wanting to explain, he dove into another question. "What about you?"

"I'm here with my son Vinny," she pointed to a small boy running in circles with another kid around the perimeter of the room. "I like the exercise and always hope it'll get some of his energy out but that never seems to happen."

He thought back on the day before and how Audrey hopped from one activity to another—each new thing only hyping her up more. "Doesn't look like he'll calm down any time soon."

Leslie widened her eyes in mock surprise. "Lucky me. Listen, I don't usually do this, but would you want to grab a cup of coffee or something some time?"

The quiet, hesitant way she asked made him rub his hand over his short hair. The spikey strands tickled his palm. He didn't want to hurt her feelings, but he had no desire to get coffee with anyone other than Elizabeth.

"Tucker! Come get teacake now," Audrey said, running over and saving him.

Elizabeth followed with a tight smile. "Hello, again. I'm Elizabeth." Instead of offering her hand as Tucker had, she rested her palm on his arm. "Sorry to steal this guy, but we've got a big date next door for some coffee cake."

Leslie kept her sunshine expression in place, but a light dimmed in her eyes. "Sounds fun. My son and I need to get going too. See you guys around."

Elizbeth didn't move her hand, instead she gave him a little squeeze. "We can skip the bakery if you aren't feeling well."

All the pain from earlier evaporated. Elizabeth said they had a date, and whether she was trying to save him or really wanted to date him, he didn't care. "I'm fine, but I need to grab my wallet from my truck first."

He ushered her to the front of the studio, offering the busy

Zoe a wave before sliding on his shoes and opening the door for Elizabeth and Audrey before stepping outside.

Gray clouds blanketed the sky and muted the morning sun. A slight breeze stirred the air, but not enough to cool his warm skin.

"You were pretty focused in there," Elizabeth said as she fell into step beside him, Audrey running just a little bit ahead. "Like a real pro. Must have been tough with such a captive audience."

He groaned. "Talk about awkward. Zoe could have given me a heads up there'd be so many women in there."

She laughed. "The class is Mommy and Me. What did you expect?"

"I expected to stand in the back corner and not be noticed."

"Trust me. No way you can be in a room full of women without being noticed. I mean, you even had an admirer. I hope I didn't cramp your style."

The hard tone of her last sentence stopped him. "Did that upset you?"

Halting, she faced him and met his stare head on. "Maybe."

The side of his mouth lifted. "Maybe I like that it upset you."

She struggled to hide a smile. "Maybe we should talk about that." Her face fell and she dropped her gaze to her feet. "I wanted to bring up some stuff last night, but it wasn't the right time. I'd like to make time. Before we figure out who's upset about what, it's important to lay all our cards on the table. With my life the way it is, I can't afford for there to be misunderstandings."

There she was. The bold woman who spoke her mind and didn't hide from anyone. The woman he'd fallen head over heels for the moment he saw her. And she was right. Their past was too complicated not to wade through it, and their present too important to leave anything up to chance. "I'd like that."

"Mommy, look!" Audrey shouted. She'd climbed up the side of the truck and pressed her nose against the passenger side window.

Tucker jogged forward, erasing the short distance between them. "What's going on?"

"It's a present!" She squealed and jumped back to the side-walk. "Come see, Mommy."

Frowning, Elizabeth clutched Audrey's hand and molded her close to her legs. "What is it?"

Tucker peered inside. "Looks like a white pastry bag from Crawley's Confection. Did Bob leave this for us?"

Confused, he opened the door and the scent of vanilla hung heavy in the cab. Then he saw it. A white scrap of paper tossed on the seat. He moved slowly, careful not to touch anything, and read the words scrawled across the sheet.

My favorite treats for my favorite girls. We'll be together soon.

15

T ucker leapt out of the truck and extended his arms, as if to shield Elizabeth and Audrey from an unseen threat. Not wanting Audrey to sense what had happened, he struggled to stay calm. "Let's head straight to the bakery. No need to hang outside any longer than necessary. It's so dang humid and looks like it might rain."

Wide-eyed, Elizabeth picked up on his tension and turned Audrey in the opposite direction. She kept her grip firmly on her daughter's shoulders. "Good idea."

"But what was in the truck? Looked like a present. Was it for me?" Audrey tried to swing around as she shot off her questions, but Elizabeth kept her pointed forward, weaving between the pedestrians walking down the sidewalk.

Tucker eyed each person who passed. Someone had gotten into his truck and left another creepy note and token for Elizabeth. He had to call the police and fill them in. The window of time where they'd been in the yoga studio was small. The person might still be around. Watching their interaction. Wanting to witness Elizabeth's response. The burning sensation on the back of his neck told him that was true, and he needed to get Elizabeth and Audrey out of harm's way as fast as possible.

"But it smelled like vanilla," Audrey protested. "Was it a cupcake? Those are my favorite."

Tucker swallowed the uneasy sensation creeping up his esophagus. He hadn't looked inside, but he'd guess Audrey was right on the money.

Elizabeth reached the bakery door and yanked it open, practically shoving Audrey inside. She steered her toward a four-person bistro table in the corner, away from the window and anyone who may be lurking outside. "Sit here, honey. Tucker and I'll order you that cupcake."

Her mouth dropped. "A cupcake before lunch?"

Tucker couldn't help but laugh at her disbelief.

"Just this once," Elizabeth said then tilted her head toward the counter. "Let's take a look at what all they've got."

He followed her to the front of the store, nerves a mangled mess, and grabbed his phone to send a quick text to Cruz to meet him right away. He kept an eye on Audrey. She was close enough for him to get to if needed but far enough not to overhear any conversations she shouldn't be around.

"Tucker! There you are." Mrs. Crawley emerged from the backroom. Her round glasses emphasized her milky, blue eyes and gray hair was worn down in a short bob. "How did your girls like their cupcakes?"

Tucker frowned. "Excuse me?"

The older woman cocked her head to the side, smile unwavering. "The cupcakes you asked me to put in your truck. With that sweet little note. Though I don't understand why you needed to say you'll be together soon. These must be the girls, and goodness, they're already here. Did they surprise you?"

"Oh my God," Elizabeth said under her breath.

"Mrs. Crawley, I never called you." Tucker spoke slow, not wanting to confuse the poor woman any more than she clearly was. "I need you to tell me everything about the phone call you received."

Mrs. Crawley furrowed her brow. "Well, the call came in about thirty minutes ago. He said it was you and wanted two vanilla cupcakes with extra frosting placed in your truck with the note on the seat."

Elizabeth rubbed a hand over the base of her neck. "He knew where you parked your vehicle. He knows we're in Pine Valley. He knows your name, and who to call to get my daughter's favorite treat."

The skin on her neck turned an angry red and he snagged her fingers, gently pulling her hand away before she rubbed herself raw. "We're going to figure this out. No one is going to hurt you or Audrey."

"Mrs. Crawley, did the man sound like me?" he asked, turning his attention back to the concerned bakery owner. "Was there any noise in the background? Did he say anything else besides asking for the cupcakes?"

She bit into her thumbnail and shook her head. "Not that I recall. But I wasn't really paying attention. The call came in when it was packed."

"Does your phone show the name and number of incoming calls?" he asked. Maybe they'd luck out and something was left behind even without the perpetrator stepping foot inside the bakery.

Mrs. Crawley's face lit. "Yes. Hold on." She hurried to the back room and returned seconds later with a cordless phone. She pushed a few buttons then handed the phone to Tucker.

"Perfect," he said, snapping a photo of the number with his own phone before returning it. "If we're lucky, Cruz can trace this. Hell, we can call and see if anyone answers."

Elizabeth nodded. "It's worth a shot, but we should wait for Cruz before making any kind of move."

"Oh goodness," Mrs. Crawley said. "I'm so sorry I let this happen."

Elizabeth offered her a small smile. "It's not your fault. You thought you were doing a favor for a friend."

"Mommy! Can I have my cupcake, please?" Audrey yelled from the corner.

Mrs. Crawley leaned to the side to get a better look at her impatient customer. "Is that your daughter?"

"Yes, ma'am. That's Audrey. And I'm Elizabeth." She lifted her hand over the glass counter.

"So nice to meet you, dear." Mrs. Crawley captured her hand then covered it with her free palm, holding her in place for a few beats. "How about I give your little one her dessert while you two talk? Is that all right?"

"I'd appreciate that."

Tucker waited while Mrs. Crawley plucked a cupcake from a cake stand and placed it on a small white plate and rounded the counter, settling at the table with Audrey.

Audrey connected her gaze with Elizabeth, seeking some kind of unspoken approval. Elizabeth gave a small nod. Audrey grinned from ear to ear as she sunk her teeth into the giant pastry.

"I can't believe this keeps happening. This guy's smart. He knew enough not to show his face to anyone but could still get what he wanted. Oh, God. Do you think he knows we're staying at the retreat?"

The fear in her eyes had him pulling her into his arms, holding her tight. He ran a hand over the back of her head, soothing her the only way he could while standing in the middle of a bakery with her daughter nearby. "We just need to be careful. He attacked me yesterday when I was by my truck. He might have just saw it in town and acted impulsively. Let's hope that's all this was."

She nodded against his chest and gripped the back of his shirt in a clenched fist.

A bell above the door rang, and Cruz walked inside. He met Tucker's eye and a small grin ticked up one corner of his mouth.

But Tucker didn't move. Didn't release Elizbeth as she clung to him. He held her tight and nothing in this world would ever make him let her go.

~

SOMEONE CLEARED THEIR THROAT, making Elizabeth pivot toward the door.

Cruz stood with a small smile on his clean-shaven face, his ever-present cowboy hat in his hands.

Tucker tightened his hold on her, clearly not wanting to let go, so she slid one arm around to hug the back of his waist. "Thanks for coming, Cruz," she said.

He took a step forward, but before he could say a word, Zoe rushed inside. She pressed a quick kiss to Cruz's cheek. "What's going on? I saw you three rush past the studio and y'all didn't look too pleased. Now Cruz is here. Did something happen?"

Tucker draped his arm over Elizabeth's shoulder. He skimmed his knuckles up and down her bare bicep. "Someone left something in my truck. He called the bakery and pretended to be me."

Zoe's eyes widened and she reached for Cruz's hand.

Elizabeth glanced over at Audrey, halfway through her cupcake. "I hate she's involved in this. Even if she doesn't realize what's going on. I don't know how long I can shield her. How long she can ignore the tension constantly surrounding us."

"You're an amazing mom." Zoe crossed the room and pulled her into a hug. "She's happy and enjoying everyone around her. Just keep doing what you're doing."

Elizabeth sniffed back tears, the words of her new friend more needed than she realized. "Thank you."

"Now, it looks like she's almost polished off her treat," Zoe said, releasing her. "How about I take her with me to the studio while you guys discuss what happened? Then you don't have to whisper or be afraid she'll overhear anything."

"That'd be great," she said, releasing a long breath.

"Good. I need help cleaning up after class." Zoe winked then hurried over to Audrey, crouching low and speaking to the girl, who gave an excited squeal and jumped to her feet.

"Mommy!" Audrey said, running toward her at the only speed she had—fast. "Zoe asked me to help her. Can I?"

"Sure, honey. Just make sure to tell Mrs. Crawley thank you first."

Audrey zipped back to the bakery owner and gave her a big hug before taking Zoe's hand and heading for the exit. She waved at Elizabeth. "Thanks, Mommy. I love this place."

The words warmed her heart and she held on to the flicker of pure happiness on Audrey's face before she was forced to deal with reality.

Once the duo disappeared out the door, Cruz motioned toward the closest table. "Wanna take a seat?"

She sighed. "What I really want is for all of this to be over and life to go back to the way it was."

Tucker stiffened.

She aimed a slow smile his way. "Almost the way it was."

Grinning, Tucker pulled out her chair then took the seat beside her. "Mrs. Crawley, can you join us for a second? I know you already explained what happened, but I'm sure Cruz would like to hear what you have to say."

Mrs. Crawley wiped the table where she'd sat with Audrey and grabbed the empty plate. She retold the story as she ferried the dish behind the counter and checked the display case. "Like I told Tucker, there's not much else to tell."

"Can I see the phone you used to take the call?" Cruz asked.

"You bet." She carried it over just as the bell chimed and a cluster of patrons entered the bakery. "I'll be right with you folks," she called, then turned to Cruz. "Do whatever you'd like with it. I need to help my customers." She squeezed Elizabeth's shoulder before greeting the family of five that waited to place their order.

"The number's on the phone," Elizabeth told Cruz. "We thought about calling it back but wanted to wait for you."

"Appreciate that." Cruz fiddled with the cordless phone. "I think it's best if I place the call. If this guy's dumb enough to answer, I don't want him to think he can reach Elizabeth with another stunt like this. And Tucker, I can't trust you to keep your cool."

Tucker trapped her hand on top of the table and nodded.

Cruz pressed a button on the phone then the placed the device between them on the table. A deep V formed in the middle of his forehead.

Knots tangled her stomach, and the sugary scents she normally loved smelled sour. The line rang, the sound echoing against the cream-colored walls.

Tucker squeezed her hand, his gaze glued on the phone as if he could will someone to answer.

A click indicated the call had gone to voicemail. Disappointment sagged her shoulders. A sinister laugh vibrated from the speaker. The sound grew louder, more fanatic before silence smothered the laughter. Heavy breathing took its place followed by a long beep, indicating the message was over.

Her body shook and numbness filtered through her limbs. This wasn't real—couldn't be real.

"He planned on us calling," Cruz said, disconnecting. "He recorded a voicemail message to screw with us."

Tears sprang to the corners of her eyes. The threats and little gifts left for her to find were bad enough, but this? The maniacal cackle filled her with a new kind of fear. Fear that didn't just revolve around a criminal breaking into her world or ending her life, but the realization that whoever was after her and Audrey could do a lot of harm before this was all over.

"Can you trace the number?" Tucker asked.

"Yeah, but chances are it's a burner. Someone this organized had a plan. My bet is tracing the number will lead nowhere but it's worth a try."

"Are Audrey and I safe at the retreat?" The thought of leaving her little secure haven almost sent her into a tailspin. She'd found a sense of peace hidden among the tranquil spot in the mountains. She didn't want to leave.

Cruz scratched his jawline. "It's hard to say. He knows Tucker's truck and his name, two things that wouldn't be hard to find out if he hung around town for a couple days. Doesn't mean he knows where he works. Where he lives. I'd say the retreat is still the best spot. Lots of eyes around to notice something. Lots of people with training to help protect you and Audrey."

"I agree," Tucker said.

She sucked in a steadying breath. "Have you found anything out about the men on the list? Talked to Caleb?"

"I spoke with Caleb last night. Claims he had the morning off the day of the shooting and spent it rehabbing the house he and his wife just bought."

The news didn't make her feel any better. "So no alibi?"

"Nope. No one was with him. He wasn't happy with the questioning. Defensive and put out. A combination that usually points to righteous indignation or alarm at being discovered."

She hung her head. "I don't know where to go from here. I feel so lost...so frustrated. How am I not seeing something that has to be right in front of me?"

Tucker tucked his thumb under her chin, and she lifted her gaze to meet his. "No one sees a monster who always wears a mask. Especially when you didn't know he was even there."

She closed her eyes, absorbing his words and knowing he was right. But this used to be her job and she'd been damn good at it. Why was she failing so miserably?

Because Cruz had been right before. She was too close.

Tucker's phone vibrated in his pocket, and he leaned to the side to fish it out. "It's Brooke. I'm going to take this really quick." He accepted the call then pressed the device to his ear. "Hey, what's up?"

All she could hear was a rapid-fire chatter from the other end, but the hardened set of Tucker's jaw and fire that lit his blue eyes told her something was very wrong.

"I'll be right there." He disconnected and climbed to his feet. "We have to get back to the retreat. Now. Someone broke into the kennel."

16

For the first time in the last couple days, Tucker wished Audrey would stop hurling questions at him as he drove back to the retreat and rushed them toward the kennel. To help pick up the pace, once they'd arrived, he'd hoisted Audrey onto his back and jogged as fast as he could. Elizabeth stayed in step beside him, the tight lines of her face reflecting his own worry.

If he found out someone hurt even a hair on one of his dogs, he'd lose his shit.

When the kennel came into view—a miniature replica of the log-cabin styled lodge—he slowed and tried to swing Audrey to her feet.

She tightened her grip around his neck, nearly choking him. "Keep running," she said through her giggles.

He shot Elizabeth a pleading look. They'd moved so fast after the call about the break-in they hadn't discussed how to handle this, but it wasn't a good idea for Audrey to walk into the kennel without knowing what waited for them. Unfortunately, he also didn't know how to tell the girl no.

"Why don't you come to me?" Elizabeth asked, extending her arms for Audrey to climb into.

"I don't wanna," she said, squeezing harder. "I want Tucker."

As much as her words warmed his heart, he needed her to get down so he could check on his animals.

Brooke rounded the corner of the kennel with her cream-colored mutt by her side.

"Another puppy!" Audrey's screech nearly destroyed his eardrum and caused the ache in his head to spike. She jumped to the ground and ran to Brooke.

"Does everyone around here have a dog?" Elizabeth forced an airiness to her tone that told him she was joking, and he loved her for trying to keep things light.

But it didn't help. His nerves were on edge.

He lengthened his stride as he moved forward. "Are the dogs hurt? Where's Otto?"

Brooke rumpled the top of Audrey's head then aimed weary brown eyes his way. "The dogs are fine. Otto's inside. The pups are all riled up and he's pacing up and down the aisle, sniffing every square inch he can find."

"What the hell happened?" He rubbed the back of his neck, torn between getting the details from Brooke and seeing his dogs were okay with his own eyes.

"Don't say bad words," Audrey chided. She stood beside Wyatt and scratched behind his ears.

He struggled to keep his composure. "Sorry."

"Izzy took a couple of the dogs for a walk. She locked up and set the alarm. Someone smashed through one of the panes of glass on the front door and let themselves in, but clearly didn't anticipate setting off an alarm in the middle of the day. By the time Lincoln and I arrived, whoever had broken in was long gone."

"Where's Lincoln now?" Elizabeth wrapped her arms around Audrey, resting her forearms on Audrey's tiny shoulders and clasping her hands just below her chin.

"Inside. He's checking over the security footage. Seeing if he can identify anything about the man that stands out."

Anticipation shot through Tucker. "You got the guy on video?"

Brooke nodded but screwed up her face. "Yes, but not a good picture of him."

"Might be enough for me," Elizabeth said. "I need to watch it."

"How about Audrey and I stay out here with Wyatt and walk by the lake?" Brooke asked, aiming a sweet smile at the little girl. "Too much excitement inside for my old boy, and I bet he'd love to chase some sticks into the water. You think you can throw some in the lake for him?"

Audrey bobbed her head up and down like a fishing lore. "Yep. Tucker taught me to throw balls."

"Great," Brooke said, holding out a hand for Audrey to grab. "We'll stay right in front of the kennel." She aimed the last part at Elizabeth, who dipped her chin in gratitude.

With Audrey distracted, he jogged to the building that housed the therapy dogs. Loud barking penetrated the thick walls.

Elizabeth tensed at the door.

"You don't have to come inside. You can watch the security footage from a different monitor."

She drew in a shaky breath. "I'm fine. I trust you, so I trust your dogs. They're probably better behaved than Audrey."

He swept open the door, allowing her to enter first.

Lincoln sat at the counter, hunched over the computer screen. He glanced up, a grim set of his mouth showcasing his frustration. "Sorry, man. Didn't expect he'd show up here. I have Grace leading a couple men through the woods. She wants you to grab Otto and meet her out there. Otto charged at the guy when he came in and got his scent. She wants to see if he can pick up the scent outside."

"Who's Grace?" Elizabeth asked while she moved behind the counter and peered over Lincoln's shoulder.

"She works here," Tucker said. "Veteran. Best tracking skills in the tri-state area. If anyone can find someone running through these woods, it's her. I'll calm the dogs then find out where she is and if she still wants Otto and me to join her."

He pushed open the door that separated the front lobby-like section from the rest of the building and Otto sprinted toward him, jumping up on his chest. The eight other dogs secured in their pens howled in welcome. Tucker rubbed Otto's head then took a step back so the canine's front paws landed on the tiled floor. "Okay, guys. Everything's fine."

He spent the next fifteen minutes reassuring his furry friends. Heaping attention and extra treats on each of them until they all laid down, exhausted from the unexpected disruption to their day.

Otto disappeared through the doggy door that led to the front of the building.

Tucker checked everything over one last time then hurried out front.

Otto had his nose to the ground and scoured the floor.

The sight of his dog so on edge twisted Tucker's gut, but he knew better than to try and make him stop. Otto sensed an intruder and he'd been trained to search him out. Halting that process would do more harm than good.

Lincoln switched places with Elizabeth, who now sat in the chair perched in front of the screen. Her eyes were narrowed, and she tapped the tip of her fingers against the counter. "Pause."

Lincoln clicked on a few keys to do as instructed.

Tucker maneuvered so he could see the screen.

"Can you zoom in?" she asked.

A few more clicks and the image grew larger. The feed was in black and white and a bit grainy. A man stood at the threshold, the glass already shattered and leaning forward slightly to snake his arm through the window. He wore a black hoodie, the hood over his head and the bill of a baseball cap pulled low over his face—which was tilted away from the camera.

"What do you see?" Tucker squinted and studied the screen, trying to find what had caught Elizabeth's attention.

She pointed at the left bottom corner, and all the color drained from her face. "You see that sliver of material poking out of his pants pocket?"

Lincoln nodded.

"What is it?"

She rummaged through her purse and pulled out an identification card with multi-colored lanyard looped through it. An eagle's head dotted the fabric in a repetitive pattern, as if in place of polka dots. "It's the same. We use them at work. All faculty members are given one for our IDs. Whoever broke into the kennel either works at the college or purchased this on campus."

Tucker balled his fists at his side as anger poured through his veins. He was pissed at such an invasion to a place that meant so much to him.

Pissed someone had the balls to show up in the middle of the day to mess with him and what he loved most in this world.

But as upset as he was, a thrill raised the hairs at the back of his neck. Their suspect list just got a whole lot smaller.

AN HOUR LATER, sweat beaded on Tucker's forehead and his T-shirt was plastered to his chest. Dirt and other debris from the forest were smudged across the bottom half of his jeans. Otto panted, in need of water, and disappointment hung over the makeshift search party as they made their way back to the lodge.

He stomped up the wide porch steps and hurried over the threshold, a primal need to be close to Elizabeth and Audrey drumming through him with every step. They'd been safe with Brooke, Mia, and Chet—safer than if they'd accompanied him in the woods—but not having them near felt like he was missing a part of himself.

Otto ran inside and made a beeline for the seating area set up in front of the fireplace. Elizabeth, Brooke, and Audrey sat on the floor, surrounding the coffee table and playing some kind of game. Mia and Chet occupied the couch, sitting side-by-side with their hands folded together. In any other situation, they made a cozy scene. But not now.

Not when a man lurked among them, pushing the boundaries and becoming bolder by the minute. Tension sizzled in the air, and even Audrey seemed uptight with her back straight and a frown on her pouty lips as she stared at playing cards clustered in her hands.

"Looks like the gang's all here," Grace said, bypassing him to snag a spot on the couch on Mia's other side. She practically collapsed against the supple suede and stretched her lean legs ahead of her.

Mia picked a twig from the long, dark braid thrown over Grace's shoulder. "Any luck?"

Grace shook her head.

Skirting around the group, Tucker settled into the oversized chair angled toward the hearth, behind where Elizabeth sat cross-legged on the floor. He leaned forward and gave Elizabeth's shoulder a reassuring squeeze before settling back in the soft chair. "Elizabeth, this is Grace."

Grace gave a nod of acknowledgment.

"Nice to meet you," Elizabeth said.

"Same."

An awkward silence covered the room, and Elizabeth kept her gaze on Grace as if waiting for her to say more. But Tucker knew she'd be waiting awhile. Grace was about as giving with her words as Chet, preferring the woods and her solitude over anyone's company.

The dull ache in Tucker's head from earlier morphed into a constant roar, partly from the rigorous hike and partly from needing a glass of water.

As if reading his mind, Chet stood and towered over them. "I'll grab you guys something to drink and a dish of water for Otto. Do you need anything else?"

"Water's perfect," he said.

Audrey met Chet's gaze and widened her hazel eyes. "Can I have lemonade?"

Chet lifted a corner of his mouth, barely perceptible through his bushy beard. "Sure. Why don't you come help me? Maybe we can add a plate of those cookies we made yesterday."

She turned to Elizabeth for approval.

"Go ahead."

"Yes!" Fisting her hand, she pulled her elbow back in an excited gesture than scurried to Chet's side. She held his hand and pumped her legs quickly to keep up with him as they made their way toward the kitchen.

"Okay," Elizabeth said once Audrey was out of earshot. "Did you find anything?"

Grace rested her forearms on her knees and sighed. "Not a lot. I followed the trail I'm pretty sure he took. I think he parked near a mountain road that runs through the property. Lincoln took pictures of the tread marks we found in the gravel and went straight to the station to try and identify the tires. Other than that, the guy's a ghost."

"Then how do you know the tire marks were from him?"

An amused smirk puckered Grace's face. "Trust me."

Elizabeth's back went rigid. "I hope you'll forgive me, but I don't know you. I don't know who to trust right now. All I know is someone is out to get me and my child and I'd like to know whatever details you can provide. So please, can you tell me how you know the man who broke into the kennel parked a vehicle on a mountain road in the woods?"

Grace's smirk transformed into a full-blown smile, clearly liking the challenge and the chance to brag. "I detected faint footprints near the kennel and followed them to a narrow trail in the woods. The prints veered off into a dense thicket of trees, where fresh breakage was found on multiple branches that led toward the road. Once we got to the gravel, the dust was unsettled and the marks fresh. Not to mention Otto's nose. He was the only canine in the kennel who wasn't locked up and got a good scent of the man we're after. You might not trust me, but always trust that dog's nose." She tilted her head at Otto, who laid on his side on the cool stone around the fireplace.

"So this guy knew where I was staying and how to park a vehicle out of view and walk right up to the retreat." Elizabeth fell back against Tucker's legs. "What do I do now?"

He had an idea, but he wasn't sure how she'd receive it. He should wait until they had a moment alone and discuss it, but they needed to act fast. If she didn't like what he had to say, then they could all come up with a different plan. "You shouldn't stay here."

Brooke frowned. "I understand you're upset about what happened, but we can keep her and Audrey safe. We'll be on alert. Let all the staff know what's going on and what to look for while Lincoln and Cruz dig in deep to the men Elizabeth works with. Just give them a little bit of time and they'll nail this guy."

"I have all the confidence in the world that they'll figure this out, but we can't sit around and wait for the next bad thing to happen."

Elizabeth swiveled to face him. "What's my other option? I

can't go home. We already discussed how a hotel isn't safe and traveling to my parents out of state isn't a good idea. So where do we go?"

He licked his dry lips, and nerves danced in his stomach. "You'll come home with me."

17

Tucker's suggestion for Elizabeth and Audrey to stay at his home gave her an immediate sense of relief . . . and made her cheeks heat. Being so close to Tucker was a temptation she didn't need, but she wouldn't pass up his offer of protection. Even if being near him and not touching him killed her. But standing in front of his log cabin tucked deep into the woods had anxiety rushing back. She offered him a hesitant smile as he opened the door. "Are you sure this is a good idea?"

Tucker widened his eyes and shrugged as if he wasn't sure of a darn thing. "We'll find out."

With her usual exuberance, Audrey ran past them and stopped in the middle of the living room. "It's a mess."

Tucker cringed and placed a hand on the small of her back to usher her in.

"Audrey," Elizabeth chided. "That's not polite to say to our host and friend." Although she understood her daughter's sentiments as soon as she stepped inside.

The house was open and airy, the living room and kitchen area one big space. A flatscreen television that was twice as big as hers was mounted above a fireplace in the living room with all the deep, brown furniture facing it. A multitude of windows showcased the amazing views, the green-tipped mountains reaching for the afternoon sky enough to steal her breath.

But it was the kitchen that had stolen her daughter's attention. Walnut cabinets were hung with no doors, and a large island sat on mahogany floors. No countertops were installed, and dust coated most of the surfaces she could see from just inside the threshold. Exposed brick lined the wall that expanded from the living room into the kitchen, a choice she wouldn't have expected but that worked in the unfinished space.

Tucker set her and Audrey's bags at his feet. "Sorry. In the middle of a remodel that never gets finished."

"No problem. I don't care to be in the kitchen much anyway." Although she wouldn't mind being in his. Puttering around to make Sunday morning waffles or cooking a simple dinner on a busy weekday evening. She could envision the space, white marble countertops with hints of gold throughout the stone and bronze brushed handles. She'd replace the off-white refrigerator with stainless steel and add a matching gas stove and dishwasher.

She blinked, washing away the image. This wasn't her house and that wasn't her kitchen. She and Audrey were guests, and hopefully only for a night or two while Cruz and Lincoln tracked down a criminal.

"Me neither," Tucker said. "I eat most of my meals at the retreat or the Chill N' Grill. I wouldn't cook much even if this was finally the way I wanted it."

"The Chill N' Grill?" Audrey scrunched her nose and dropped to her knees on the sage green rug to get closer to Otto. "What's that?"

"Only the best restaurant around. Maybe we'll order there tonight. The owner, Wade, can drop it off."

"Sounds perfect. Where should we put our stuff?"

"This way," he said, recapturing the handles of the bags and rolling them down the hall. "There's the bathroom. Feel free to put whatever you want inside. Plenty of space. That's my room," he said, tilting his head toward a closed door to her right then motioned toward two closed doors on the left. "And here are the two guest rooms. You can each have your own or you can share."

A part of her wanted to take her own room and enjoy her space—something that hadn't happened for days—but the larger part of her wanted to keep Audrey close. "We'll share thanks."

"Then take this one. It's a little bigger." He opened the door and waited for her to enter before placing her bags by the door. He lingered in the doorway.

"This is beautiful." She wasn't sure what she'd expected, but it most certainly wasn't the cream-colored eyelet comforter over the wrought-iron bed. A powder blue armchair rested in the corner with a round white end table beside it. Black and white photos of the mountains hung on the walls.

"Thanks, but I can't take the credit for decorating. My mom treated this house like her own personal project after I bought it. She'd stop by every day with paint colors and fabric swatches. As if I cared what it looked like. I just wanted a comfortable place to crash with a big yard for the dogs. I like to bring some home with me every now and again. They need space to run."

She'd never asked him about his family. From years before, she'd known he was an only child and his dad had passed away when he was in high school. But she hadn't even thought about asking after his mother. "Does she live close by?" She wanted to add that she'd love to meet the woman who'd raised such a kind-hearted and thoughtful son, but she didn't want to terrify him.

Tucker dropped his chin. "She died a couple years ago. Suffered a stroke."

Sensing his emotion, she wrapped him in a hug. "I'm so sorry. Loss is never easy, even if years have come and gone."

He snuggled her close. "At least it was quick for her. She didn't suffer. But I miss her every day. That's part of the reason I haven't finished the kitchen. It will never get her stamp of approval or have her flair. I'm afraid that once it's done, every time I see it, I'll regret not making exactly what she would have wanted."

"I'm sure all she ever wanted was your happiness. No matter what that looks like."

He pulled back, his face so close to hers she could see the tiny specks of gray in his eyes. He studied her face, his mouth slightly parted as if having something to say yet unsure of how to say it.

"What is it?" she asked, the desire to know every part him moving her closer.

The side of his mouth hitched up. "She would have liked you. Liked what you stand for. How you treat people. You're impossible to resist."

She licked her lips, unsure if he was speaking about his mother or him, and God help her, she prayed *he* couldn't resist her. Because she couldn't stay away from him a second longer. She was tired of guilt and fear holding her back. She wanted him to finally see how much he'd come to mean to her—how much he'd always meant to her.

Energy crackled between them, and he lowered his mouth toward hers.

She closed her eyes, her pulse racing.

"Mommy!" Little footsteps pounded down the hall, accompanied with the clacking of Otto's nails.

Tucker jumped away with a lazy grin.

She pressed a hand to her rapidly beating heart, willing it to slow. Being on the run, away from her home and ripped from her normal life had been tough. But nothing would hold a candle to wondering what Tucker's lips tasted like while he slept across the hall.

TEN MINUTES LATER, Tucker took a step onto his back deck and inhaled a deep breath of fresh mountain air. Leaning forward, he gripped the top of the railing enclosing the large structure that jutted into the woods. He'd cleared land on the side of his home to give the dogs the space they needed, but he hadn't changed one thing about the expansive yard behind his house. Hell, he'd even kept the old maple tree, choosing to build his deck around the ancient trunk instead of chopping it down.

A shallow stream trickled down a slight incline that ran away from his property. The sound of water lapping over the rocks calmed his nerves. Birds chirped in the trees and the gray skies combined with the canopy of leaves to make the day appear later than it was.

His mind spun in a continuous loop, replaying the moment he'd almost kissed Elizabeth. She'd been so close, her lips right in front of his. And now he had to keep his cool and pretend like she hadn't just rocked his world as he spent the next few hours with her and her daughter.

The sliding door screeched open, and Audrey bounded outside, Otto attached to her. "Wow. This tree's awesome." She hopped onto the bench he'd built around the tree and reached for the lowest limb.

Chuckling, he lifted her up just enough for her fingertips to grasp the branch.

She swung back and forth like the cutest monkey he'd ever seen. "Can we take a walk? Mommy said we could find new trails yesterday and it never happened."

He glanced skyward. The idea of getting out of the house was appealing, but the weather wasn't promising. "Looks like it might rain."

She hopped to her feet on top of the bench, bringing the top of her head to his chest, and shrugged. "So. I won't melt."

"Fair point," he said, unable to argue against her logic.

The door slid open again, and Elizabeth stepped outside. She'd thrown a thin cardigan over her pink tank top and a sexy glow illuminated her makeup-free face. "What's going on out here?"

"I want to take a walk. You said we could take Otto."

"I think it might rain. Feels like it too. Temperature dropped and the wind's starting to blow."

"She won't melt," he said, struggling against a grin.

"I wonder who told you that." She aimed raised brows at Audrey then met his eye. "Okay, we can take a short walk, but I don't want to wander far."

Her meaning was clear—the weather wasn't the only reason for staying close to the house—and he gave a brief nod. "Sounds good. Let's just explore the backyard a bit. There's plenty to see, and we can walk along the stream a little. It's super shallow and sometimes I find frogs hopping along the shore."

"Yay!" Audrey ran for the stairs, waiting for them to follow, before sprinting down to the lawn.

Tucker fell into step beside Elizabeth while Otto and Audrey ventured a little ahead. He loved watching her discover the most ordinary things. Picking up a heart-shaped leaf, pointing out a ladybug on an old stump, and laughing at a pair of squirrels that argued over a fallen acorn. Things he'd never stopped to appreciate. Things he'd never overlook again.

Elizabeth stayed close to his side as she sidestepped branches and jumped over rocks.

Tension sizzled in the space between them. He replayed the

moment he'd almost kissed her over and over in his mind, wishing he could go back and have one more minute to finish what they'd started. To finally taste those full lips and feel her body pressed against his.

The wind picked up, scattering debris across the forest floor and causing tiny ripples to flow along the water. But the movement of air did nothing to beat back the flames burning inside him. Damn, he needed a cold ass shower as soon as they returned to the house.

"A frog!" Audrey gasped and ran to the stream. Water splashed up her legs, and she crouched low for a better look at the fat frog squatting on a rock in the middle of the narrow waterway.

The frog jumped into the water and hopped away.

Audrey giggled and took a few steps toward it before something else caught her attention.

"Are you sure the water doesn't get any deeper?" Elizabeth asked.

"Nah. I call it a stream because I don't know what else to call it. The land slopes downward and this trickles in a constant flow. Makes for a pretty view, but nothing more."

"Perfect for a rambunctious kid who can't help but dive headfirst into what she finds."

"Yeah." A pinch of sadness tightened his gut. Now that he'd witnessed Audrey laughing and playing with Otto in his space, the idea that she might not be here long squeezed his chest. The ache unlike anything he'd ever known.

"What's wrong?"

He blew out a long breath, loving and hating how well she could read him at the same time. "I like having you both here. A lot."

She smiled and held his gaze. "We like being here."

His heart pounded an unsteady rhythm. He might not be as good as Elizabeth at figuring out what people were thinking, but he was tired of not asking questions. Time had long past to just move from moment to moment and see how things played out. He wanted Elizabeth, and he needed to be positive she had no doubts about where his intentions lay. "I don't want to go back to the way things were. I've missed you like hell the last few years. Missed hearing your laugh and seeing you smile. Discussing cases and sharing small details about our lives. We were friends, and I hate that we lost that."

She shifted her gaze to Audrey, who collected pebbles and stuffed them in her pockets. "After we buried Gary, I lost myself preparing for motherhood. Once Audrey came, I shut out the world. Even my own parents, who constantly hounded me to move from the town Gary had once called home. I'm all Audrey has, so I gave her 110% all the time. And there was no way to do that if I was constantly reminded of what happened—if I lost myself in my grief and fell apart. That little girl needed me too much for that."

Her words stung, but he understood her position. She'd had too much on her plate to allow anything else in her life. But now, all he wanted was to help ease her load. To be that partner she'd said she wanted. "And now?"

She faced him again. "The last few days have shown me how little I have in my life besides my daughter. She will always be my number one priority, but I need more. I need friends. I need a community. I need you."

Her confession sucked the air from his lungs, but he still wasn't certain of what capacity she wanted him in her life. Not like it'd matter. Whatever she asked of him, he'd give her and Audrey. Even if that meant just a friend who lent a helping hand—a storyteller to keep the memory of Gary alive for all of them. Because Audrey wasn't the only one who needed to be reminded of who Gary was. They all did.

"You have me, Lizzie. You always have."

Her grin widened. "You really know how to make a girl swoon, don't you?"

He barked out a laugh. "Not sure anyone's ever said that before."

Taking a step forward, all amusement vanished. He slid his palm around the base of her neck, letting his fingers get tangled into her hair.

She stared up at him with wide eyes, her bottom lip tucked between her teeth.

Not wanting another interruption, he erased the distance between them and placed his mouth on hers. Aware that Audrey was close by, he moved his lips slowly, savoring the sweetest moment of his whole damn life before breaking away.

Her chest puffed up and down and a warm glow tinted her cheeks.

A sprinkle of rain filtered through the trees and splattered on the ground. Circles dotted the stream, expanding and overlapping one another until they were replaced by new drops of water.

Audrey squealed. "It's raining!"

Capturing Elizabeth's hand, he laughed at Audrey and gave a shrill whistle for Otto to heel. "Don't worry, girl. You won't melt, remember? But we better hurry up before it starts coming down any harder. Let's go home."

18

The scents of greasy burgers and French fries hung in the air even as Tucker finished cleaning up dinner while Elizabeth worked at getting Audrey to sleep. A bone-deep exhaustion tightened his shoulders, but nothing could stomp out the anticipation swimming in his gut. Audrey had remained the center of his and Elizabeth's attention after the rain interrupted their walk. With the little girl in bed, he hoped to finally lay all his feelings at Elizabeth's feet.

Needing to calm his nerves, he secured two stemless wine glasses and filled one with a dry white, wine. He grabbed the bottle and both glasses and headed out to the deck.

This was his favorite time of day. When the night settled in around him and the sounds of crickets and toads echoed off the star-riddled sky. The rain had gone, and fireflies danced in ribbons of space where trees and overgrown foliage didn't dominate the forest beyond his deck.

He selected the swing big enough for two close to the door and placed the bottle and extra glass on the small table at his side. Taking a small sip, he pushed his feet against the floor and lost himself in the gently swaying motion as he went over all the things he wanted to say to Lizzie.

Lizzie.

He'd called her by the nickname he'd always used earlier, and for the first time in years, it hadn't made her angry. She'd smiled, then let him kiss her.

His bare toes curled against the smooth wood, the memory forever ingrained in his mind.

The door opened, and he watched Elizabeth step over the threshold and slide the door close behind her.

"She finally go to sleep?" he asked.

"Yeah. Otto kept messing with Kitty, like he was looking for a treat hidden inside the stuffed animal or something. Audrey was getting all worked up, but I finally calmed both girl and dog down."

He scratched his chin, frowning. "Weird. Otto has toys, but he never goes after anything in the house that isn't his."

"Something tells me you don't have a lot of stuffed animals laying around the house that aren't for him," she said with a wicked grin.

"You got me there."

A contented sigh floated from Elizabeth and she approached the railing, gazing out toward the horizon. "You keep telling me how I'm great at reading people, but you have the most uncanny habit of reading my mind."

Amused, he picked up the empty glass and bottle of wine and moved to stand beside her. "What do you mean?"

"Since the first day I stepped inside the lodge at the retreat, all I wanted was to enjoy some good wine on the deck and enjoy the view. This is perfection."

He tipped the bottle, filling the glass half full before handing it to her. "The view of the mountains isn't the only thing that's perfection."

The twinkle lights strung around the deck showed off the

slight blush of her cheeks. She accepted the wine and took a sip, letting her eyes shut for a beat. "Thank you for this—for giving us a minute to just sit and relax and pretend like nothing evil is happening away from here."

He shrugged. "You don't have to keep thanking me. These last few days, with you and Audrey in my life, have shown me everything I've been missing. Everything I want."

She was silent for a beat, her attention fixed ahead and a timid smile spreading across her face. "It's been eye opening for me as well. For multiple reasons."

"Which are?" he asked, giving a teasing tone to his words.

Smirking, she cupped her free hand on his bicep before heading to the swing he'd just vacated. She took another long drink of wine then patted the spot beside her.

He forced his feet not to sprint to her and settled back in his seat. The warmth of her body combined with the humid air and sweat coated his palms.

"Watching you with Audrey has shown me she needs a strong male role model in her life. I can see how much she admires you. I can't be her everything anymore."

Not knowing what to say, he set his glass beside the bottle of wine and draped his arm over her shoulder. "You're an incredible mother. Audrey is beyond lucky to have you. I've enjoyed getting to know her and hope to stay in her life in whatever way you both want me."

"If it were up to Audrey, I don't think she'd ever go back home," she said with an indelicate snort.

The idea of Audrey remaining a permanent fixture in his life pressed his heart against his chest, but what about Elizabeth? Telling her he wanted nothing more than for them both to stay would scare the shit out of her. As much as he loved the picture that created, it was too soon. "I'm sure that would make Otto the happiest dog on earth. The dog's going to suffer a broken heart when he doesn't get to see her every day."

"We've all suffered enough brokenness to last a lifetime." Her words floated on the air in a whisper.

"I don't want you to suffer. For any reason. I want to be a part of your life too, Lizzie. If you'll let me."

She stared up at him with wide, round eyes. "I want that, too. I can't go back to the way things were. I can't shove the memory of you aside and try to forget all these feelings. Not anymore."

Taken aback, he furrowed his brow. "What do you mean?"

She blew out a shaky breath and stared down at the glass cradled in her palms. "I tried to bury all my memories of you along with Gary. It was too hard to remember the laughs we shared and friendship we'd built. The three of us spent so much time together. And the more I thought about you in those early days after Gary died, the more I craved your companionship. Which meant the more guilt swallowed me whole. I mean, how could I yearn to spend time with you after what happened? After Gary was dead and I'd had his child?"

Her admission sucked the air from his lungs. He'd always assumed she'd pushed him away because of her anger with the role he'd played in Gary's death and nothing more. "You needed a friend. And Gary would have wanted us to be there for each other—for me to be there for Audrey. Hell, all he ever cared about was making people happy. He'd have done anything just to see your smile, no matter who put it there."

She finally lifted her gaze to meet his and unshed tears swam in her eyes. "Do you think he'd be happy we found our way back to each other?"

Needing to know she believed him, he shifted to face her as best he could. "Gary would want you to be with someone who treats you with kindness and respect. He'd want a man in Audrey's life who would step up and love her like his own. He'd never doubt I could be that man. Hell, he's probably looking down on us right now, scheming to make sure we both know we have his approval."

Sniffing back tears, she laughed. "I wouldn't doubt it. He always loved to get his way, no matter what he had to do to achieve it."

A hundred memories slammed against him. Memories he'd ran from for so long. Memories he needed to share with Audrey and Lizzie, but not now. Not when he needed to understand exactly where her heart lay. "Did you mean what you said? About me sticking around?"

She swallowed hard and nodded. "Absolutely. I can't imagine you not in my life—in Audrey's life."

Joy expanded inside him, making tiny tingles of excitement burst in his gut. He slid his hand to rest at the side of her neck, his fingers running through the long strands of her hair, and he gently brought her face to his. Her beautiful grin was all the incentive he needed to join his mouth to hers.

A DEEP, burning desire to taste every inch of Tucker took control of Elizabeth. Damn, it'd been so long since a man had kissed her senseless.

And she wanted more.

With her lips still pressed to his, she placed her wine glass on a side table then wrapped her arms around his neck, bringing him closer. His tongue slipped into her mouth and she met it with her own, enjoying the sensation of being a woman falling in love.

A moan purred in her throat and she shifted, needing to be closer. Needing more of everything Tucker was willing to give.

He groaned and looped an arm around her back and pulled her onto his lap.

Her knees settled on either side of his thighs, her core

nestled against his as the swing rocked back and forth beneath their weight.

He roamed his hands up her ribs, his touch igniting a flame inside her. Oh God, her skin was on fire. She deepened the kiss and splayed her palms along his jawline then pulled back. The depths of blue in his eyes held so much warmth and kindness and love it almost brought tears to her eyes.

Frowning, the V between his eyebrows deepened. "Are you okay? Do you want to stop?"

She smiled, his constant consideration pulling at her heart strings. "Never. I just can't believe this is happening. That I'm here with you like this after all this time. After everything. I thought I was happy before, that Audrey was enough, but you... you've brought more into my life than I ever realized I needed."

Wonder transformed the lines in his face, and the side of his mouth hitched up with the sexy half-smile that turned her to a puddle of mush. He brought his hand to her cheek and swiped a stray strand of hair from her face before crushing his mouth to hers again.

The feel of his hard chest pressed against her breasts tightened her stomach muscles. Shallow breaths caught in her throat. The evening breeze swirled around her, doing nothing to calm the heat building inside her at a rapid rate. She pressed kisses up the side of his face then nibbled his earlobe. "I think we need to take this inside."

His body stilled. "Are you sure?"

She stared into his brilliant blue eyes and got lost in the moment. In the emotion pouring out of this man who meant so damn much to her. "I've never been more sure of anything in my life."

In one swift movement, he swept her into his arms and stood.

She looped her arms around his neck and rested her head on his shoulder as they stepped into the house and he carried her toward his room. She cast a glance toward the closed door to the guest room and said a quick prayer that Audrey wouldn't wake through the night.

Because tonight, all she wanted was to forget her troubles and worries and danger constantly knocking on her door.

Tonight, she wanted to get lost in Tucker's touch. Tomorrow would come soon enough, but for one night, all she wanted was to feel loved.

THE FIRST RAYS of sunlight filtered through the window and skimmed across Elizabeth's face. She woke with a smile and stretched her arms above her head before snuggling against Tucker, whose palm rested on her waist.

He stared at her with an easy grin. "Morning, beautiful."

Her toes curled and she burrowed closer, soaking up the scents of citrus and evergreens that always clung to him. She pressed her lips to his collarbone as memories of the night flooded her. All she wanted was to crawl on top of him and pick up exactly where they'd left off only hours before. But one glance at the clock on the nightstand told her she didn't have the luxury of lounging around in Tucker's bed much longer. "Good morning."

As if reading her mind, he tightened his grip and swung her to rest on top of him.

She giggled and gave him a quick peck on the mouth. "I have to get up. Audrey will be awake any second."

He groaned and slid his palms down her back to cup her ass. "Are you sure? I mean, she went to sleep pretty late last night."

Biting into her bottom lip, she struggled to remain focused and not surrender to the smoldering desire screaming to erupt.

The alarm screeched on her phone. She stretched to grab it

then settled against Tucker's side before opening her home screen.

He kissed the side of her head. "Why'd you set an alarm? Plan on escaping before I woke up?"

She giggled. "No, I wanted to be awake before Audrey usually gets up. Wow," she said, frowning. "I have a lot of missed text messages."

"From who? Did something happen?"

"Not a clue. I don't recognize the number." She opened the message, and a litter of photos cluttered her screen. Her heart rate ramped up and she sat up straight. "What the hell is this?"

Tucker sat beside her, leaning over her shoulder to peer at her screen.

A steady beat of fear galloped in her chest and her hand trembled as she swiped through pictures of her walking in the woods with Tucker by her side, photos of Audrey splashing in the water, and an image of her and Tucker kissing. "He followed us here. He knows where I am."

"We need to call Cruz and Lincoln now," Tucker said, hurrying out of the bed and jamming on a pair of jeans. "Then we need to get the hell out of here."

19

Tucker tightened his grip on the steering wheel as he maneuvered through the throngs of people converging in downtown Pine Valley. "I forgot about the damn parade. People are coming into town early to reserve good spots to watch. Parking is always a nightmare."

"I want to watch the parade," Audrey said, excitement drawing out her words.

Otto sat beside her in the backseat, his tongue lolling, his attention fixed on the stuffed cat in Audrey's lap.

Elizabeth cast a glance over her shoulder. "We'll see, honey." She connected a quick look with Tucker that told him there was no way they were going to the parade then stared back out the window. "Looks like all the streets are blocked off down here."

"The parking lot at the station is small and will be full," Tucker said. He slowed to a crawl until he reached the next turn. Jaywalkers clogged the streets that hadn't been barricaded. Venders crowded on the square and spilled out onto the sidewalks. "I'll find a spot to park as close as I can, and we'll just have to walk."

She nodded and tension rolled off her in waves.

He struggled to keep his emotions in check as he found an open spot and wedged in his truck. He'd had the best damn night of his life with Elizabeth in his arms only to wake up with an icy bucket of terror dumped over his head. Someone had been at his home, taking pictures of Elizabeth and Audrey, and he'd had no idea.

A fresh surge of anger pulsed through his veins, but he had to ignore it and focus on getting Elizabeth and Audrey safely to the police station. Then they could figure out what the next steps were. Crossroads was no longer safe for them, and now his home wasn't a good option either.

Stepping down from the truck, he hurried to the passenger door to spring Audrey loose. Otto waited for her to jump into Tucker's arms and get settled on her feet before leaping to the ground.

Audrey's eyes widened. "There's ice cream over there," she said, pointing to a bright pink food truck serving waffle cones filled with multiple scoops. A worker in a pink and white striped shirt leaned out the window and handed a young girl a huge cone. "I just had breakfast and that girl already has ice cream."

He had to laugh at the awe in her voice. Staying to watch the parade among hundreds of hyped-up people wasn't the best idea, but he might be able to talk Elizabeth into getting Audrey something fun to eat. Leaning close to Elizabeth so Audrey couldn't hear, he asked, "What do you think? Maybe we can get her something to snack on to keep her happy while we're at the station? Might appease her a little bit."

The first smile he'd seen from Elizabeth since she'd received the disturbing photos flashed on her face. "As long as I can get some too."

He pressed a quick kiss to her cheek. "You can have anything you want, honey."

Taking Audrey's hand, he led them through the increasing crowd. The sweet-smelling scents of elephant ears and caramel corn mingled in the air. Eager-faced pedestrians darted for long lines in search of fried food or specialty trinkets while others carried lawn chairs toward the blocked-off streets to gain the best views for the parade.

Tucker's heart thudded against his chest. He kept his eyes open and on high alert, scanning the crowd with every step. He nodded at people he knew but kept a firm grip on Audrey's hand as he pressed forward.

Elizabeth stayed close to his side, Otto next to her. They moved as one unit—vigilant and determined. He might not know what tomorrow held but one thing was certain, he would die before he let anything happen to the two beautiful ladies who'd stepped into his life and brought him more happiness than he'd ever dreamed.

The line for the ice cream was shorter than most, and he quickly found the end.

Audrey jumped up on her toes. "We're getting some?"

Grinning, he crouched down to her level. "Sure thing. Figured it's a special treat for a special girl. Then we have to go to talk to Cruz."

She frowned. "What about the parade?"

He shrugged, not wanting to lie but also hating to disappoint her. "Speaking to Cruz right now is really important, okay? I don't know how long we'll be at the police station. If we have time, maybe we can watch some of it. But if it's over before we come back outside, I promise we'll find something else that's just as much fun."

She nibbled her top lip and studied the surrounding area. "Maybe I can do that." She pointed to a square tent with a game set up inside. Dozens of fishbowls sat at different heights on plywood tables with colored fish swimming around each bowl.

Ping pong balls were being tossed in the center at all sides of the table.

He glanced up at Elizabeth and arched a brow.

She wrinkled her nose. "No fish."

Audrey sighed dramatically then aimed a smirk at Tucker. "We'll talk later."

He laughed and straightened. "What kind of ice cream do you want, munchkin?"

Audrey rolled her eyes, showing her disdain for the nick-name. "Chocolate, please."

"And you?" he asked Elizabeth.

She pressed her lips together and squinted, as if trying to solve the world's hardest math problem. "One scoop of choco-late, one vanilla."

Audrey's jaw dropped. "You get two scoops?"

Chucking, he ruffled the top of Audrey's head and her hair stuck out in tufts. "I'll get you two scoops, too."

She grinned and hugged his legs. "Thank you!"

The couple in front of him stepped to the side with their treats, and he approached the counter and relayed his order.

The twenty-something woman handed him one cone, which he passed to Audrey, then handed him the second cone.

"What about you?" Audrey asked. "You need some, too."

He held Elizabeth's cone in his hand while she searched for napkins on the little table set up in front of the food truck. Using his free hand, he snagged his wallet from his back pocket and struggled to get cash out of the leathery folds.

A loud popping erupted into the crowd, one after another. Screams filtered into the mid-morning air. The crowd shuffled around him, terror and panic clear in every face. Fear tightened his chest.

More popping. More screaming. A handful of people fell to the ground and covered their heads. Most sprinted away, moving the crowd and everyone in it like a giant school of fish.

Audrey clutched onto his leg.

Elizabeth turned to him with wide eyes, her body frozen in place.

The cone in his hand fell to the ground and he abandoned his wallet on the narrow steel counter. He'd witnessed the glazed look in Elizabeth's eyes and her inability to move many times in his life. PTSD was a nasty bitch, and no doubt the gunshot-like-noises had triggered her after her experience at the college. "Elizabeth," he said, his voice stern yet gentle. "You're okay, but we have to go. Now."

He reached down to take Audrey's hand, but nothing was there.

Otto barked and charged into the crowd.

He spun in a circle, his heart seizing in his chest. "Audrey?"

Elizabeth snapped out of whatever haze of horror had paralyzed her. "Audrey! Oh my God, where'd she go? She was right here." She bent down and scooped Audrey's stuffed cat off the ground and hugged it to her chest.

Spying a patch of black fur weaving through the panicked crowd, Tucker took off at sprint. Elbows jabbed him as he rushed past. He shoved around the frantically moving bodies, keeping Otto in his sights.

Otto, please don't lose sight of Audrey.

Sitting in Cruz's office, Elizabeth clung to Kitty. She rubbed the soft velvety skin of its ear between her thumb and index finger, seeking comfort from the toy that had comforted her daughter. Audrey was gone. Vanished. Nowhere to be found.

What she'd survived the last couple of days was nothing compared to the horror fisting her heart. Audrey could be anywhere, with anyone, and there was no way to find her. Unless she figured out who the hell had taken her.

Otto paced back and forth across the room. His tail rigid and fur along his spine straight up.

Tucker perched on the edge of the seat beside her and squeezed her hand. His face was nothing but tight lines and a mixture of anger and terror. He tapped the toe of his sneaker against the thin carpet and kept his gaze locked on Cruz, who sat behind his desk with his phone pressed to his ear.

"Okay. Keep in touch. Thanks." Cruz disconnected the call before pinching the bridge of his nose.

A hundred questions filtered through Elizabeth's mind, but she couldn't give voice to any of them for fear of what the answers would be. Tension wound its way around her neck so tight she thought she'd die. This was her fault. If she hadn't frozen, hadn't panicked. If her mind hadn't went blank, she wouldn't have lost track of her own child—her heart outside her very own body.

"Well," Tucker demanded. "Anything?"

"Looks like someone set off some firecrackers. Small, simple ones you can find almost anywhere. My guess, the guy used it as a diversion to get to Audrey, knowing it'd cause chaos. The crowd was large and scared and ran like hell. A perfect storm to get his hands on Audrey."

Elizabeth pressed her knuckles to her mouth to stop a sob. As much as she wanted to fall apart, losing the thin grip she had on her sanity would do nothing to help her daughter. "I didn't hear her scream. Did she fight back? Did he hurt her? She knew better than to just leave with a stranger." The possibility the man responsible had hurt her child to keep her quiet made vomit shoot up the back of her throat.

Otto settled on his haunches beside her and rested his head on her lap. He pushed his nose against the soft stuffed animal and sniffed.

"What if she knows him?" Tucker asked. "Then she might have walked away with him because she was scared. Could be someone she trusts. Someone she might have even been excited to see."

"Elizabeth," Cruz said. "I know this is difficult, but who would Audrey walk away with? Who would she believe was here to see her and would make her feel safe and secure leaving you behind?"

The identities of all the men they'd discussed spun through her mind. Instinct tightened her gut. "Audrey's a people person. Very trusting. Hell, she walked away with the woman at the park to get ice cream. But after that happened, we talked about not leaving with strangers and using our code word before going with anyone other than me."

"Does anyone else know your code word?"

She swallowed hard. "Courtney."

"Call Courtney," Tucker commanded, attention on Cruz. "Find out where she is. Where her husband is. Either one could have bought a lanyard from the college, and both know more about Elizabeth and Audrey than anyone else. Either, or both of them, makes the most sense."

Bile sloshed in her stomach, and tears pooled at the corners of her eyes. She blinked to make them disappear as she struggled to keep up with Tucker's words. "Courtney would never hurt her. Never hurt anyone. And there's no way she attacked Tucker outside his truck. She can't be behind this."

"She could be working with her husband," Cruz said. "You might not want to see it, but maybe there's a deeper motive than we realize. Maybe the real target has been Audrey all along—for both of them. We need to speak with the sitter and get some answers before we cross her or her husband off our suspect list."

"I'll call her," Elizabeth said. She needed to do something tangible to help get Audrey back, and she couldn't stomach the idea that the young woman she'd trusted with her daughter's life could've play any part in the nightmare she now found herself.

She plucked her phone from her pocket with trembling fingers.

Otto whined and shoved Kitty to the floor, gluing his black nose to the fabric.

She swiped the stuffed animal away and held it close. She needed the soft toy to make her feel closer to Audrey. Otto went back to his original spot with his head on her lap, as if needing the same thing. The line rang and she ran her hand over Otto's head. Each second that passed heightened the hysteria tightening her chest.

"Elizabeth!" Courtney gushed as soon as she answered. "How are you? Is everything okay?"

The question caught her off guard and she connected her gaze with Tucker's.

Concern radiated from his every pore, and he squeezed her hand. She let out a long breath and tried to steady her nerves as she refocused on her call. "I'm fine," she lied. "Just wondering where you and Caleb are."

"We're actually driving," Courtney said, a weird note in her tone. "Caleb was getting drained with all the home renovations, and I've been on edge worrying about you and Audrey. We thought it'd be a good idea to get away for a night or two. I'm so sorry, did you need me? I didn't think to check in with you first. You said to take a few days off until things settled down."

A flurry of emotions rattled her insides, and she struggled not to crack. "Oh, that's nice. I didn't need anything. Just checking in. Where are you guys going?"

"Caleb found a darling little cabin close by. Nestled in the woods. He rented it for two nights. If you need me to come back though, all you have to do is ask. I'm here for anything you or Audrey need."

"I appreciate that. Have a good time." She ended the call

and let her eyes fall shut. She'd hoped to get off the phone and know without a shadow of a doubt Courtney had no hand in any of this shit. But the sinking feeling inside screamed she hadn't seen who her sitter really was, and maybe she'd invited a monster inside her home.

20

The hesitant cadence of Elizabeth's sitter's voice rang in her ears as she jumped out of Tucker's truck and sprinted to Courtney's front door, Audrey's stuffed animal still firmly in her grip. Only Courtney's blue sedan sat in the duplex's driveway—Caleb's SUV nowhere in sight. Maybe Courtney hadn't lied about leaving town, but she'd held something back. And the nagging voice inside Elizabeth's head screamed to find out what hadn't been said.

Because finding out what was said between the lines just might lead her straight to Audrey.

"You sure you know where she keeps a spare key?" Tucker asked, coming up behind her. "Not like I wouldn't bust through the damn door if it meant finding Audrey. I'll just need a better cover story for Cruz if this involves breaking and entering."

His commitment to helping her find her daughter melted a bit of the icy fear gripping her heart. All she'd had to do was tell Tucker she wanted to search Courtney's apartment and he'd brought her here. No questions, no argument, just complete trust in her instincts and soul-crushing desire to do whatever she could to find Audrey.

"I have a spare on my keyring. She brings Audrey here sometimes, and Audrey has a knack for leaving her stuff. Courtney thought it'd be easier for me to have a key in case I ever need to run over and grab something Audrey forgot." Her mind wandered to just a few days ago when Audrey had left Kitty and refused to sleep without her new toy. What would happen tonight if they didn't find her? Would she sleep without her animal? Would she be scared and cold and alone, wondering when she'd go home?

No. She couldn't go down that path or she'd slowly lose her mind. All she could do was concentrate on the next step, the next move or plan. She rummaged through her bag and secured the keys, shoved the jagged piece of metal into the brass knob and turned it in one swift movement.

The door swung open, revealing the dark living room/kitchen combo and nothing but an eerie silence.

"No one's here," Tucker said, escorting her over the threshold and closing the door behind them after Otto ran past. "But that doesn't mean something inside can't point us to where they are."

"She keeps her computer in the guest room. Maybe there's an email or cyber trail to follow."

Elizabeth didn't bother with the lights as she ran down the short hall and turned into the guest room. A twin bed, dresser, and small desk took up the cramped space, and she plopped down on the desk chair and powered on the computer.

"Did either of them take classes at the college where you teach? The video of the man in the kennel showed the keychain from the school. You confirmed it was the same one given to the faculty, but could Courtney or Caleb have purchased one on campus?" Tucker poked around the room, sliding open the closet door and picking around coats and dresses.

"Courtney took a few classes. That's how I found her. She was attending school for early childhood education, and I put an ad in the paper for a sitter. We hit it off right away, and it was clear she adored Audrey. She's worked for me almost two years now." A flash of memories played in her head of all the times Courtney had shown Audrey love. Kissing her scraped knee at the playground, buying her ice cream on her days off, and tucking her in at bedtime so Elizabeth could catch up on paperwork. Had all that been a lie? A ruse to gain their trust so she could snatch away her daughter?

Tears clouded her eyes, and she blinked them away. She couldn't get sucked into the panic and questions. She needed to focus. Rubbing her fingers over the soft material of Kitty, she grounded herself as best she could. The screen morphed from black to blue before asking for a password.

"Does she still take classes?" Tucker asked, breaking into her thoughts.

Otto trotted to her side and placed his head on her lap. A quiet whine hummed from his throat.

"No," she said, shaking her head and searching her memory for a good password to unlock the computer. "After she and Caleb got engaged, she dropped out. She wanted to plan the wedding then start a family right away. She'd asked to keep watching Audrey while she had her own kids. I liked the idea of Audrey having little ones around, almost like siblings. I thought the plan was perfect, but now I'm second-guessing everything."

Tucker slid the closet door back in place and crossed over to the wooden dresser that was painted a dull gray with white flowers. "Did Courtney mention if she'd had difficulty conceiving? If so, would that make her more possessive of Audrey?"

The idea was like a punch in the gut, and Elizabeth struggled not to get sick all over the keyboard. She tried to push aside the emotion and only let the facts and logic filter in. "I never would have thought so, especially since they hadn't been trying long. A lot of couples can take years to conceive."

She tried a few passwords—birthdays and the name of

Courtney's first pet—but nothing worked. With shaking fingers, she typed in Audrey's birthday.

Nothing.

A puff of relieved air leaked from her mouth, and her shoulders hunched forward. "There's also the issue of all the notes talking about 'his girls' and us being reunited. If Caleb wanted to take Audrey, why would his notes include me as well?"

Closing the top drawer, Tucker shrugged then opened the next one. "I don't know. Maybe 'his girls' was in reference to Audrey and Courtney. Maybe it never had anything to do with you."

It was possible, but the explanation didn't sit right with her. All her training, as well as every instinct in her body, screamed that she was at the center of this. "What about Paul being shot? Your theory could work—even with the attack on you if it was Caleb and he was warning you to stay away from Audrey—but that doesn't play with Paul's murder."

Tucker let out a long breath and scrubbed a palm down his face. "I don't know. Maybe I'm just grasping at straws because I want it to be them. Because if not them, then who?"

She understood his frustration. Finding themselves at a dead end wasn't an option right now. Taking another stab at the password, she typed in Courtney and Caleb's anniversary and the home screen came to life. "I'm in."

Tucker leaned over her shoulder and read through the icons on the desktop. "Bring up the web browser. Most people don't log off their accounts."

She did as instructed, and Courtney's inbox popped up. She scanned the emails, but nothing told her where the couple had gone.

"Try the sent folder. Maybe she mentioned something to Caleb that gave him the idea to rent a specific place."

"Good idea." She clicked over and the third email down caught her attention. She opened it and fell back against the chair. "She sent an email to a friend with an ultrasound attached. Courtney's pregnant."

Mumbled curses tickled her ear, and Tucker dropped to the side of the bed. "Would a pregnancy make her more or less likely to do something like this?"

"I don't know," Elizabeth said, her soul quivering. "And I have no idea how to find out."

RAGGED BREATHS TRAPPED inside Tucker's tight chest, making it hard to draw in air. He struggled to keep his shit together. He had to be strong for Elizabeth, not break down into a blubbering mess because he felt absolutely helpless. He'd never known fear like this, and the fact he was powerless made him want to shove his fist through a wall.

A wailing sob sounded from Elizabeth and snapped him out of his own pit of despair. He jumped to his feet and erased the distance between them. He threw his arms around her and held her close, wishing he could absorb all her pain and terror. "We're going to find her. I promise you."

She pulled away and shook her head, and the tears streaming down her face tore his already aching heart in two. "How? We don't have a clue about where she is or who took her. We don't know if she's cold or scared, hungry or alone. Is she close? Has he taken her so far away I'll never see her again?" Another round of sobs shook her shoulders, and she hung her head.

He smoothed a palm over her back, searching for the right words to say but nothing could make things right. Could stitch her back together. Until he found Audrey and brought her home. "Honey, listen to me. Give yourself another minute to break down and let out everything. I'll hold you as long as you need. But then we're going to pull ourselves together and we're going to figure this out."

"We've been chasing our damn tails for days. That's not going to change with a snap of our fingers and sheer will." She drew in a shuddering breath then straightened, using the heels of her hands to wipe at her face.

Red splotches marred her fair skin, and he used the pad of his thumb to tuck a strand of hair behind her ear. "We can do anything. You and me. Together. But first, we need to shut off the computer and get out of here. Then we'll talk to Cruz again and we'll find her. We'll find Audrey." He pressed a kiss to her forehead and waited for her to make the first move before standing.

Otto jumped to his feet and glued himself to Elizabeth's side.

Elizabeth rubbed his back and clutched Audrey's toy tight.

Otto whined and gently nipped at the stuffed cat.

As if she didn't have the strength to keep her grip on the plushie, she released it and let Otto take it in his mouth.

His tail stood straight, and he gently held it like he would a puppy.

And Tucker's heart shattered all over again.

A dull vibration came from Elizabeth's cross-body bag, and she dug inside for her phone. A pale sheen beat back the redness in her cheeks, and her mouth dropped open. "It's a text message from the same number that texted the photos."

He frowned, his blood pounding through his veins. "More pictures?"

"A video. Oh my God, I'm going to get sick."

He slid behind her and kneaded her shoulders. "You got this, and I'm right here with you." He kept his gaze trained on the screen, not wanting to miss a second.

She pressed the play button and lifted the phone for them both to see clearer.

Pink walls and a room filled with frilly toys and feminine furniture took over the screen. Stuffed animals were scattered over the neatly made bed. Elizabeth gasped. "That's Audrey's room."

Squinting, he studied the video. Sure enough, the same rocking chair he'd sat in after Elizabeth's house had been broken into was tucked in the corner and the shaggy cream rug anchored the room.

A loud squeal announced a bouncing, giggling, twirling Audrey. She stopped mid-spin and stared at the camera and waved. "Hi, Mommy. I'm having so much fun! Come play with us." She ran away, the sound of her laughter echoing behind her before the screen went black.

"She's at the house. We have to get her. Now."

She didn't give him time to dissect what they'd just seen before she ran from the room. He followed behind her, a million questions flitting around his brain. He didn't bother to lock up as he sprinted to the truck, opened the door for Otto to jump in the back, and settled in the driver's seat.

Audrey being taken back to her home didn't make an ounce of sense, but he couldn't deny what had been right in front of his eyes. He just had to figure out how to slow Elizabeth down before she rushed headfirst into a trap in order to save her daughter.

21

A combination of anxiety and adrenaline pumped through Elizabeth's veins and tightened every muscle in her body. She sat ramrod straight on the edge of the bench seat in Tucker's truck. The scenery on the short drive from Courtney's duplex to her home flew by in a haze of colors and shapes, a single thought registering in her mind.

Get to Audrey.

Tucker disconnected the call he'd been on. "Cruz agrees taking Audrey back to your house then sending a video of her asking you to come over and play doesn't make any sense."

"None of this makes sense," she snapped then pinched the bridge of her nose.

He rested a hand on her thigh. "I understand you're upset. But we can't just charge into your house and hope to get Audrey out safely. Elm Ridge PD is on their way."

For once his touch didn't calm her, his words did nothing but irritate her. "You don't understand. Audrey *is* my whole heart—my entire world. I can't just sit back and wait. Knowing she's in the house."

"We're not sitting around and waiting. We've taken the right steps and done everything we should. I know this is an impossible thing to ask, but just for a moment, try and take yourself out of the situation and look at this from the point of view of a former FBI agent. If the location of a missing child was given, who should be called? Who takes the lead? Would you allow the parents to rush in and take over, hoping things go smoothly? Or would you trust the trained professionals to do their job?"

She squeezed her eyes closed and struggled to keep a firm grip on her spiraling emotions. The vehicle jostled to the side, cluing her in that Tucker had made the turn toward her home. Toward Audrey. She wanted to argue with him, but he was right. The only thing that mattered was getting her arms around her baby girl, and she'd do whatever she had to do to make that happen.

She forced her eyes open. "I'm sorry. You're right. But I think this guy's plan is pretty clear. Use Audrey as bait. He knows I'll come running, no matter the risk to my own safety. So he goes to the house, makes her feel secure, then lures me there. I'm sure he has everything set up the way he wants it, has used the space to his advantage, or is planning to continue to use Audrey to cover his own ass."

Tucker tightened his jaw, and she had no doubt the thought of Audrey being used for someone's sick and nefarious purposes bothered him almost as much as it did her.

"Agreed. He has to know you won't come alone. That you'll have me and police with you. The only way he can possibly get you and Audrey, as well as himself, out of that house, is to threaten to hurt either of you until he gets away."

"If I see or hear anything that makes me think Audrey's in danger, I won't wait for the police," she said, forcing as much steel as possible in her tone. She'd gladly rush in without anyone behind her, take a freaking bullet if it meant keeping Audrey safe.

"I wouldn't ask you to, and I'll be right by your side if we go in there. I'm going to park a few doors down so he doesn't see us approaching," he said, turning onto her street.

"Good idea." Unhooking her seatbelt, she tapped her foot against the floormat and prepared to leap out the door. "Then we'll split up. You take Otto to the back yard, I'll go to the front. See whatever we can that we can convey to the police when they get here."

"No," he said, voice firm. "We stay together. We stay under the radar and wait for backup."

She swallowed an argument because his plan made too much sense. As much as she'd gladly trade places with Audrey to get her out of harm's way, getting all of them out alive was the goal. "Fine."

Tucker pulled onto the side of the road and cut the engine then took her hand before she could fly out of the vehicle then grabbed his gun from the glove compartment. He didn't plan to enter the home, but he'd rather be prepared just in case. "Remember. We stay together. I'm here with you and for you. Always. Now let's go get Audrey."

A lump wedged in her throat, and she fought to keep unshed tears in her eyes. Love bloomed in her heart, but now wasn't the time to say it, to confess her feelings. So instead, she pressed her lips to his then breathed in the scent of him to ground herself as much as she possibly could when her world was broken into pieces.

HEAT from the afternoon sun beat down on the back of Tucker's neck as he nestled his Glock into the back of his jeans.

Otto stood beside him and waited for a command. It'd been years since the dog had been put to work, been expected to perform in an operation of any kind. But he'd picked up on the tension, understood what was at stake and Tucker knew Otto would do anything he could to help Audrey. Tucker's job was to make sure his companion didn't do too much, no matter the outcome.

Blowing out a long breath, he stared hard at Elizabeth. "Ready?"

She nodded. "We should loop around this house now and stay hidden."

"Let's go."

He let Elizabeth take the lead, Otto close to her heels while he brought up the rear. He kept his ears tuned to every snapping branch or rustling of leaves. He ducked behind trees as he crossed through the neighbor's lawns, hoping not to be spotted. Anxiety knotted his stomach, but he had to push it aside.

Coming to the edge of Elizabeth's yard, she hesitated and glanced over her shoulder. Her eyes were wide with fear. "Are you ready?"

He nodded once and secured his gun in his hands.

She licked her lips and ran her hand over Otto's head.

The idea of Otto comforting Elizabeth warmed him more than the boiling sun, but he had to keep a level head right now. Not get sucked into the tenderness watching Elizbeth and Otto created inside him.

Staying low, she sprinted past the cluster of evergreens that bordered her yard and around the wooden swing set. He and Otto kept close. His heart pounded in his ears. Images of his last mission threatened to paralyze him, but he beat them back. Gary's death wasn't his fault, and he'd do everything in his power to make sure Elizabeth and Audrey didn't meet the same fate.

Elizabeth crouched behind a shrub.

He stayed close behind her.

"Lights are off," she said. "Doesn't look like anyone's inside."

Squinting, he studied the windows on the back of the

house. No curtains blocked the views. "I agree, but we can't be too sure."

"This is torture. She could be right there, right on the other side of that wall. I mean, how long does it take the police to get here?"

The stillness of the house set him on edge. Intuition trickled down his spine. Something wasn't right. "Let's head to the front. Keep out of sight as much as possible."

Staying in the shadows, they rounded the side of the house. No noise penetrated the home. No shifting or creaking or anything else to announce that someone was inside. After finding a spot to stay hidden behind a towering Maple, Tucker studied the surrounding homes. "Does your neighbor have a security system?" He pointed toward the corner of the house next door where a camera was situated.

She shrugged. "Looks like it. I don't talk to them much, so I've never asked."

A car in the driveway signaled someone was home. "I'm going to see if they'll let us check the footage. The angle of the camera should catch your front door."

They took off for the house, Tucker taking the lead. He hurried up the driveway and down the brick sidewalk, pounding a little too hard on the front door.

An older man with thinning hair and stooped shoulders answered. Confusion rippled along his wrinkled brow. "Can I help you?"

"Sorry to disturb you, sir. I'm here with your neighbor." He nodded toward Elizabeth, who gave a small wave. "Her daughter is missing, and we have reason to believe she may be inside her home. The police are on their way, but could we watch your security footage to see when the suspect brought the child to the house?"

The old man blinked in horror. "Yes, please. Do whatever you need. My grandson insisted I set up this pesky feature on my phone. I can bring up the video feed right here for you." He grabbed his phone from a holder on the side of his pants and pressed a few buttons before passing it over.

Tucker accepted the device and quickly oriented himself to the program. He selected the time lapse button, allowing the feed to speed through until he found what he wanted.

But nothing showed up on screen. No one came to the door. No vehicles entered the driveway.

"I don't understand," Elizabeth said as she pressed close to watch the footage. "No one has been here. I don't have a door in the back. Besides access to the garage, which no one has entered, there's one way in and one way out."

"Thank you, sir. We appreciate your cooperation." Tucker handed back the phone.

"Good luck. I hope you find her." He offered a kind smile before disappearing inside.

A gleam of determination lightened Elizabeth's eyes. "I'd bet my life no one is in that house, and I won't stand by a second longer and wait to find out."

Securing her keys in her hand, she ran to the home.

Damnit. He might agree with her conclusion, but he didn't agree with her plan. Either way, he couldn't let her enter the premises alone. He and Otto quickly caught up as she unlocked the front door and quietly inched it open. "I'll go in first," he said, gun in hand.

He stepped softly onto the wood floor. Sunlight filtered into the room. No laughter floated from the hall. No chatter or drone of the television livened up the space. The hum of appliances drifted from the kitchen.

He tiptoed forward. Elizabeth stayed close, Otto even closer. They moved together and made sure no one hid in the kitchen.

"Head toward her room," Elizabeth whispered in his ear.

He moved down the hall. His tennis shoes squeaked against

the floor, and he tensed. Waiting for someone to charge toward him. When nothing happened, he pressed on.

The door to Audrey's room was closed. He pivoted to Elizabeth and lifted a finger, signaling her to wait. He held his breath and pressed his ear to the door, hoping to hear anything that would clue him into what was going on inside.

Nothing.

His core tightened. He'd been around Audrey almost nonstop the past few days and the girl never quit talking. No way she was quietly sitting in her room playing.

Unless she was sleeping. Or worse, injured.

Unable to wait a second longer, he lifted a sweat-slicked palm to the handle and cracked open the door inch by inch until it stood wide open.

And Audrey was nowhere to be found.

22

The wail of sirens matched the keening in Elizabeth's soul. Her house was empty. No sign that Audrey or anyone else had been there. She sat in the rocking chair in Audrey's room with Otto beside her and her heart crumbled into dust.

Panic paralyzed her. Her mind was numb. A tiny voice inside her head told her to get off her ass and do the next logical step.

But she couldn't move. Couldn't think. Couldn't begin to use logic in a world that was completely upside down without her baby girl in her arms.

The scream of the police vehicles died down and the faint click of car doors closing penetrated the haze of fog around her. She should get up, let the officers inside and fill them in on what happened. But Tucker was there. He could handle that while she pulled herself back together.

She just had to figure out how.

Muffled voices were followed by slow footsteps toward her. She stayed in her spot and kept a hand firmly planted on Otto's head. The dog offered her more comfort than she'd thought possible. His heart obviously as broken as hers.

A soft knock brought her focus to the doorway. Tucker took a step inside the room and Lincoln hovered in the hall, the grim set of their mouths showcasing their frustration.

"I'm so sorry," Lincoln said.

She stared at him, unable to even dip her chin to acknowledge his words.

Tucker shoved a hand through his hair. "Cruz is pouring over notes and files back at the station, trying to find whatever the hell we're missing. Other officers are still tracking down witnesses from the parade and hoping someone saw something that could help."

"Can I see the video that was sent to you?" Lincoln asked.

She let her eyelids fall closed for a brief second and allowed herself one more moment to feel the crushing blow of pain pounding against her entire body.

Otto's whine and the feel of his head in her lap opened her eyes. She dug down deep for what little strength she had left and unlocked her phone. Watching the video again would be like daggers to the heart, but she needed to see her baby girl's smiling face and study the scene again. Because if anyone would notice anything of importance in the video, it was her.

The phone bounced in her unsteady hand, and Tucker crossed the room. "Here. Let me hold that."

Lincoln stood beside him.

A sense of comfort swept over her as each man flanked her chair. Both silently offering whatever support they could.

Tucker pressed play and held the screen where they all could glimpse the video.

Audrey's face came into view, and Elizabeth sucked in a hard breath. Tears sprang to her eyes, but she forced herself to look beyond her sweet girl. Now that she knew Audrey wasn't in her room, she noticed small differences. A thin crack on the wall by the window. A stain on the carpet in the corner. No pink bin beside the closet with toys spilling out everywhere.

The video ended and Lincoln cleared his throat. "I can see why you thought she'd be here. The rooms are identical."

"Someone went through a lot of trouble," Tucker said. "Do you think he's so concerned with making Audrey feel comfortable he'd create a replica of her entire room?"

A chill turned Elizabeth's blood to ice. She'd seen this type of behavior before, in smaller, less terrifying measures. "It's a product of his obsession. Of his firm belief that Audrey and I are a part of his family. He doesn't just want her or me. He wants our entire life."

"I agree," Lincoln said. "He's wrapped up so tight in his own twisted reality, he honestly believed you'd go to her. To the home he shares with the two of you. I wouldn't be surprised if this place has more similarities to your home. But one thing we know for sure, whoever took Audrey has been in your house multiple times."

Flopping back in her seat, she rested her elbow on the armrest and let her head fall in her palm. "We also know he had a key. He could have let himself in at any point. The person didn't have to be invited. He's made sure to take whatever the hell he wants, when he wants it."

Tucker rounded the chair and dropped to a crouch. He took her hands in his and swiped his thumbs over her knuckles. "We'll find her."

Anxiety gripped her chest. If Audrey wasn't with her tonight, healthy and happy, she didn't know what she'd do. How she'd live. She took her phone back from Tucker and stared at the frozen image of Audrey smiling on her phone. She prayed her daughter really was smiling and playing at this moment, with no idea the danger she was in.

Realization dawned on her. She turned in the chair to stare up at the men. "Her kitty."

"What about it?" Lincoln asked. He maneuvered so he stood in front of her and frowned.

She played the video again. The stuffed animal she loved so much rested on the bed. "That's not Kitty. Kitty's in the truck. She had her toy with her when he grabbed her, and she dropped it. Someone made sure she had another Kitty."

Tucker tightened his grip. "Shit. How did we miss that? How long has she had the stuffed animal? Who all knew she carried it with her?"

"She's only had it about a week. So Courtney knew. Audrey left it at her house one night and wouldn't sleep until I ran over and grabbed it. I mentioned it to Ed the other day when he came to work exhausted. Didn't sleep much because his son lost his blankie and cried all night."

"We talked to Ed," Lincoln said. "He'd gone to visit his parents in Kentucky. Spoke with his mom. Unless he came back to town without us knowing, he's in the clear."

"Did you buy the toy for her?" Tucker asked.

She shook her head. "Sebastian bought it. Her birthday was coming up and he said he wanted to be the first to give her a present."

The memory of her coworker gifting Audrey the plushie sent a tidal wave of little moments slamming against her. Sebastian remembering Audrey's birthday, Sebastian knowing Audrey's favorite kind of pizza even though they'd never shared a meal, Sebastian poking his head in her office and seeing Paul giving her a hard time before the fire alarm sent him scattering outside to his death.

"Otto," she said, straightening and staring down at the dog's soulful brown eyes. "He's been relentless about Kitty since yesterday. After the kennel was broken into. How long would a stuffed animal keep a person's scent?"

Tucker clenched his jaw. "Close to two weeks. Sonofabitch. Otto recognized the scent on the toy from the kennel. We need to call Cruz and find out what he's uncovered about Sebastian Tillman. I bet my life he's the asshole who took Audrey."

MINUTES LATER, Tucker and Lincoln sat around Elizabeth's kitchen table to find an alternative location for Sebastian. The Elm Ridge PD were on their way to Sebastian's house on the other side of town. Tucker understood Elizabeth's need to be in the action, to be the first face Audrey saw when she was found, but chances were low Sebastian had taken Audrey to his house.

At least to the residence where they'd quickly found an address.

This guy was too smart, too prepared, to lead them to his doorstep. He and Lincoln were both convinced the authorities would show up to Sebastian's house to find no one home. They needed to uncover everything they could about him and pray it led them straight to him and Audrey.

Elizabeth paced around the table with her phone pressed to her ear. "Okay, thank you. Yes, please call if you think of anything else." Disconnecting, she sank down on the distressed wooden chair. "That was Mindy, who I work with. She hasn't spoken with Sebastian and claims she doesn't know him too well."

Lincoln sat across from her and scrolled through his phone. "Cruz sent over everything he's found so far. He'd concentrated his search on Ed so there's not a ton yet, but he did petition the Department of Defense to get ahold of both Ed and Sebastian's records. He's calling now to explain the situation and hopes they'll speed things up since a child's in jeopardy."

Elizabeth flinched.

"What about the woman who was at the campus with Sebastian when we were in your office?" Tucker asked, grasping at straws. "She mentioned he walked her to her office. Maybe she knows him a little more and could offer some insight."

"I'll call her." Elizabeth leaned against the back of her chair. Bags hung low under her eyes. The heavy load she carried on her shoulders was broadcasted in every line of her face.

Tucker pulled his seat next to her, wanting to give her strength and comfort any way he could.

"Hi, Elizabeth," Lindsay said, her voice clear and upbeat through the speaker. "How are you doing?"

She found his gaze, as if seeking guidance as to how to handle the question.

"Tell her everything," he whispered. They were past time playing things close to the vest. Elizabeth needed to let this woman know exactly what happened in case she wanted to keep anything to herself.

"Not good. Audrey is missing."

A sharp gasp boomed into the room. "What? How?"

Elizabeth gave the short version of the story, starting with her assumptions over Paul's death and ending with her suspicions that Sebastian had taken Audrey. "You two seem close. Has he ever said anything that seemed off? Things about me or my daughter that you found odd?"

"Never," Lindsay said. "He's always been so nice and helpful."

Tucker didn't doubt the woman's sincerity, but that didn't mean she hadn't been as duped as everyone else. "Lindsay, this is Tucker. We met the other day. Has Sebastian shown interest in Elizabeth outside of wanting to be her coworker? Ever asked you personal questions about her?"

"I mean, I guess, but who doesn't ask questions?"

"What kind of questions?" Tucker pressed.

"He'd ask about her work schedule sometimes, wanting to know when the best time was to ask her to hang out with the rest of the staff. When he was looking at houses a couple months ago, he mentioned a home he was interested in being near Elizabeth's and we talked about the neighborhood. Very innocent things. Nothing that shouts out he's a kidnapper or stalker."

He'd argue that point, but there was no reason.

"You said he was looking for a new house in my neighborhood," Elizabeth jumped in. "Do you know if he purchased one?"

"Umm, I know he bought something but I'm not sure if that's the one. I wish I could help more, honest I do, but I don't know anything else. I'd never suspect Sebastian of doing something so evil, and as much as I hope you find Audrey, I still have a hard time believing he's the one behind her disappearance."

Her voice took on a haughty, no-nonsense tone that raised Tucker's blood pressure. The woman hadn't shown much empathy toward Elizabeth, hadn't offered anything but excuses for the man who'd probably put her through hell.

"Thanks, Lindsay. I've got to go." Elizabeth disconnected. "We need to pull up the recent sales within the neighborhood, pressing out further into town if needed. Makes sense he'd want to purchase a home close to me and Audrey. All we have to do is find it. Lincoln, run a search for any properties listed under Sebastian's name. Chances are slim we'll find anything else under Sebastian Tillman, but it's worth a shot. Tucker, let's find any other name combination that would make sense he'd use when making a purchase. Even a relative who could have purchased the house and given him access."

Pride pushed out the pain in his chest. Elizabeth was swimming in grief, yet she'd found a way to keep her head above water and be the woman she needed to be. The tough-as-nails FBI agent who understood how to work a case and get the job done.

Lincoln quirked up an eyebrow. "Good plan. I'm going to

grab my laptop from the car. It'll be easier than using my phone."

He waited for Lincoln to leave the room before squeezing her hand. "We've got a trail now. A damn good one. We'll find them."

His phone buzzed and he quickly accepted Cruz's call. "Hey, man. We think Sebastian purchased a house near Elizabeth and are trying to find the property. Do you have any information that could clue us in to an alias? Connections we could use?"

"I'll dig through everything I have in a second, but I thought you might want to know about the conversation I just had regarding Sebastian Tillman's discharge from the army."

Knowing Elizabeth would want to hear as well, he put the call on speaker and held the phone between them. "Go on."

"Turns out he was dishonorably discharged three years ago after an incident with one of the female soldiers."

Elizabeth sucked in a breath. "What did he do?"

"The Department of Defense was pretty tight-lipped about specifics, but when I pressed, they confirmed he underwent a mandatory psychiatric evaluation. There were claims of harassment that occurred after the woman he'd been engaged to had been killed by a suicide bomber overseas. Appears he snapped after her death and clung to a specific woman in his battalion. Was convinced they belonged together and manipulated situations to put himself in her path as often as possible. He finally crossed a line and was discharged."

Anger tunneled Tucker's vision. How had the college not known about Sebastian's past? How had they allowed a known predator to work at a campus filled with so many unsuspecting women?

"This fills in so many holes," Elizabeth said. "But doesn't tell us where he is."

Lincoln ran through the door, his laptop open and in his

hands. "I think I found him. House sold three months ago two streets over. The property is listed under Sebastian Pearl."

Tucker frowned. "Pearl? How did you know to search for that name?"

"It's his maternal grandmother's maiden name. Listed under an LLC. The guy might be smart, but he's not smarter than us."

Elizabeth jumped to her feet. "Give me the address. It's time to bring my daughter home."

23

L ate afternoon crept in, the sun still bright and hot against the blue sky. Air pumped from the vents in Tucker's truck. He'd parked at the end of the road, far enough not to be seen from Sebastian's house but close enough for them to keep an eye on things—for Elizabeth to rush to the scene as soon as Audrey took a step outside, and Sebastian was no longer a threat.

As though not wanting to be alone, Otto had refused to sit in the back and instead rested between her and Tucker. He sat tall, his gaze out the window.

Hours had passed since Elizabeth's world had crashed at her feet, and she prayed Audrey would be back in her arms before night fell. Hopefully, the floor plan they all studied on Lincoln's phone would help them gain a better understanding of what the officers were walking into.

"Do you think he'll expect us?" She bit the inside of her cheek, her nerves a mangled mess.

After they'd verified the address belonged to Sebastian, a plan had quickly taken shape. First, they needed to confirm he was inside. An officer would pretend to be a delivery man, and once

Sebastian came to the door, the other officers hidden around the property would sweep in, apprehend him, and grab Audrey. The plan was simple enough, but Elizabeth understood more than most that these things hardly ever went exactly as planned.

"He'll be on alert," Tucker said. "He sent the video and knows we've been searching for Audrey. He'll be suspicious of anyone who comes to the door. We have to make sure he doesn't see anyone other than the officer standing at his door with a package and the vehicle in the driveway. Even then, as long as we get a visual and know he's inside, we can move ahead."

She appreciated Tucker's straight-forward answer. The last thing she needed was someone pumping her full of false hope. She just had to trust that once things got started, the trained officers would do their job and do it well. Knowing both Cruz and Lincoln would be taking the lead untangled a few of the knots twisting her stomach.

"I wish I could be the one to go inside," she said, staring down the street at the small cottage with the white shutters and bright red door.

She'd passed this home a dozen times after the For Sale sign had left the yard, never giving a single thought as to who had purchased the home. The neighborhood was older, so it wasn't uncommon not to see anyone in the yard of most of the houses. As long as the properties were well maintained and lawns mowed, she didn't give much thought as to who lurked inside. Especially a house two streets over.

Tucker clapped a hand on her knee. "Me too. But it's smarter to let the police handle this. If Sebastian sees either of us, it might set him off. We don't want him to act erratically and do anything to harm Audrey."

A blue van with the name of a delivery service drove past them and pulled into Sebastian's driveway. Nervous energy swirled through her. She bounced her knee and kept her gaze locked on the vehicle. Everyone was in place. She couldn't see the officers in position to storm the gates, but she knew they were there. Knew they were ready.

A medium-sized man with khakis and blue polo hopped out of the van. He wore a black baseball hat and carried a package in one hand, and one of the black electronic devices to collect signatures in the other.

Elizabeth held her breath as he moved quickly up the sidewalk and stepped up to the door and rang the bell. She gripped Tucker's hand that still lingered on her leg. "What if no one comes to the door? What if there's no visual identification that moves the operation forward?"

"We can't get caught up in what ifs. Sebastian will come to the door, then officers will surround the house. Sebastian's proven he's not an idiot. He'll know there's no way around this, no way to escape."

A hundred ways this could go wrong played on repeat in her mind, but she refused to give voice to them. Refused to get sucked into the fear. So she watched and waited. "Someone opened the door." She squinted, staring through the windshield to get a better glimpse of who stood just inside the house.

But they were too far, too much between her and the cozy cottage to verify who was in the home.

Tucker's phone vibrated. "It's Cruz. He confirmed Sebastian's inside."

Tears appeared in her eyes and tumbled down her cheeks. She dashed them away. Relief mingled with disbelief. Sebastian was her coworker, hell he'd been as close to a friend as she'd allowed in her life the last few years, and a part of her brain still held out hope she'd been wrong. That she hadn't misread him all this time. Now there was nothing but cold hard facts. And as difficult as it was to swallow how much she'd missed, at least she knew where Audrey was.

Seconds ticked by like hours. Nothing more happened. No movement. No signals. No sign that the next stage of the plan had been set into motion.

"Shit." Tucker's panicked curse snapped her back to the moment.

He slid his hand away from her leg, and the absence of his comforting touch made her ache. Alarm beat back her tears. "What's wrong?" She scootched as far forward as she could, searching for what had caused Tucker's reaction.

The officer at the door placed the package on the ground and lifted his hands in the air before taking two steps backward.

Tucker called Cruz.

Elizabeth's heart hammered faster with every ring.

The line picked up.

"What the hell's going on?" Tucker demanded, not waiting for Cruz to comment.

"Sebastian's at the door. He has a gun," Cruz said, his voice eerily calm and steady. "And he's securing Audrey in front of him."

Elizabeth's mouth went dry as sweat beaded on the back of her neck. Her limbs shook, and every thought except one fled her brain.

She had to get to Audrey.

Pushing out the door she took off at a dead sprint.

"Sonofabitch." Tucker jumped out of the truck and ran after Elizabeth, Otto hot on his heels. Muffled murmurs came from his phone, and he held it to his ear. "Elizabeth heard you and took off toward the house." She hadn't gotten much of a head start, but determination and fear pushed her. Making it hard to catch up.

"I see her," Cruz said.

Cruz stepped out of a cluster of trees that bordered the property line beside Sebastian's house. He held out his arms to signal Elizabeth to stop, but she dodged him, sheer will propelling her forward.

Tucker shoved his phone in his pocket and sped forward, catching up with Elizabeth as she approached the edge of Sebastian's yard. "Lizzie," he shouted. "Wait a damn minute."

Stopping, she turned toward him. She'd set her mouth in a hard line. Her eyes narrowed. "I can talk to him. I can make him let her go. I need to get to her."

The unspoken plea in her voice tugged at his heart. "I know, honey." As much as he wanted to persuade her to stay back and let the police do their job, he knew he'd never convince her to wait in the shadows. And from where he stood, Elizabeth had a better chance of securing Audrey's safety than a yard full of officers that Sebastian found threatening. She was trained in a way no one else here was. She understood how to talk down a dangerous criminal, and Sebastian's imagined connection to her might open his mind to what she had to say.

She gave a tiny nod then faced the house and walked forward, stepping further across the yard. "I'm here, Sebastian. Let Audrey go."

Cruz wiped a palm down his face, his displeasure of the turn of events evident in his scowl. "I don't like this. She shouldn't be here."

Tucker clenched his jaw, torn between protecting Elizabeth and doing whatever it took to get Audrey away from the man who held her life in his hands. But deep down, there was no choice. Audrey's safety was priority number one. "Leave her be. She can handle this."

Cruz frowned, his hand on the butt of his gun at his side.

Sebastian stood on the narrow porch with his back pressed against the now-closed storm door. One arm was latched across Audrey's slim shoulders. He held a gun in his free hand and pointed it at the side of her head.

Anger collided with dread and made Tucker sick to his stomach.

Audrey's large, terrified eyes latched on to her mother. "Mommy. I'm scared." Her bottom lip trembled, and she sniffed.

Otto growled beside him, and Tucker placed a hand on the back of his neck. "Down, boy."

Otto sat, but tension radiated from his quaking body.

Elizabeth took another step forward, her sneakers pressing down on the green blades of grass in the yard. She held her palms in the air to show she came forward with no weapon. "I'm right here, sweetie. I won't let anyone hurt you, okay?"

Audrey nodded but the promise didn't appear to put her at ease.

"I don't want to hurt her," Sebastian said. "I love her. We've had so much fun together, haven't we? We played and danced and made lunch. I just need your mommy to come home now. And the only way to get her to come inside is to show her that she doesn't have a choice. Now, everyone else needs to leave us alone so we can spend time together as a family."

Tucker bit back a growl of his own and fisted his hands at his sides. He couldn't tear his gaze from Audrey's terrified face. A swirl of emotions tangled up his insides.

"Don't worry about anyone else," Elizabeth said. "I'm the one you want. There's no reason to have a weapon. Especially that close to Audrey. I know you love her. You don't want to hurt her. Even if it were just an accident. So why don't you put the gun down and we'll just talk?"

Tucker had no clue how she kept her voice so calm. He held his breath and waited for Sebastian's reaction. His peripheral vision caught sight of two other officers on the other side of the blocked-off street.

Sebastian snorted out a laugh and shook his head. "Do you think I'm stupid? If I put down the gun, all these assholes will come at me. Not going to happen. They all need to leave. Now. Or I'll be forced to do something we'll all regret." He tightened his grip on Audrey, and she whimpered as tears slid over her red cheeks.

Tucker lunged forward, but Cruz's hand on his shoulder stopped him.

"You and I both know that won't happen," Elizabeth said, pressing forward inch by inch. "You're smart. You planned this whole thing for months without anyone having the slightest idea. But you just made one very big mistake."

Sebastian frowned. "What's that?"

"You threatened a child in front of police officers. They can't allow that to happen. They can't leave knowing Audrey's in danger."

Her voice caught and Tucker almost fell to his knees.

A flitter of realization dawned on Sebastian's round face. He darted his gaze around the yard like a caged animal. "What do you propose I do then? We're supposed to be a family. All three of us. Together forever."

Elizabeth took one more step, putting her closer to Sebastian than Tucker standing back on the street. "Let Audrey go, and I'll come inside and make sure everyone leaves."

Terror tightened Tucker's throat. She couldn't exchange herself for Audrey. Couldn't go into the house with Sebastian. She'd never make it out alive.

The arm clasped around Audrey loosened, and Sebastian smiled. "You'd do that? You'd commit yourself to me and a life together if I let her go?"

"Yes," Elizabeth said. "You and me. We'll figure everything

out. I promise. I know you don't want Audrey to get hurt. Please. Take me instead. It's your only way out of this mess."

"Fine. If you walk inside and everyone leaves, I'll let Audrey go."

"Lizzie," Tucker called, unable to hold himself back a second longer. "You can't do this. You can't trust him to keep his word. Walking up to that porch will only put you in danger and keep Audrey in the same dire situation."

Elizbeth turned toward him, her face a mask of professionalism and calm.

But he saw the fear in her hazel eyes, the desperation in the tight set of her shoulders.

"I have to, Tucker. You and I both know I can't let her stay with him. Please, take care of her for me. Promise me. No matter what happens, you'll always love her like your own."

Before he could utter one of the hundreds of thoughts floating in his head, Elizabeth darted across the rest of the yard and stood in front of Sebastian.

He opened the storm door. "Get inside. Then I'll let her go."

Elizabeth shook her head. "No. I won't go in until I know she's safe."

Sebastian ground his teeth. "Fine." He shoved Audrey off the porch.

Audrey sobbed and clung to Elizabeth. "Don't do it, Mommy. Don't go."

Sebastian pointed the gun at Audrey, and Tucker sprinted forward.

"Take her." Elizabeth struggled to unhook the panicked girl's arms from around her waist. "Remember I love you honey. Always." She loosened Audrey's grip, spun her toward Tucker, and gently pushed her in his direction before jumping up the steps and disappearing inside the house.

24

T he image of Audrey with tears soaking her little face and her body trembling as she held on tight was burned in Elizabeth's brain as she stumbled forward into the entryway of Sebastian's house. Her heart tore in two. She struggled not to collapse in a heap on the tile floor. Her job wasn't over. Audrey might be safe, but now she needed to figure out how to get herself out of this mess.

Because if there was anything she knew with one hundred percent certainty, Tucker wouldn't give up on her.

The door clicked behind her, and she turned on her heel.

Sebastian grinned, almost sheepishly, and ran a hand over his hair. The brown strands had grown out a little and the scruff along his jawline told her that he hadn't shaved in days. "I can't believe you're really here. I know how hard it was for you to leave Audrey, but don't worry. We'll get her back. I weighed my options and getting you alone for a few days without our daughter around had too much appeal to resist."

Bile sloshed in Elizabeth's stomach, but she forced a smile. She'd kill this sick sonofabitch before she let him get his hands on Audrey again, but she couldn't let him know that. She needed to play his twisted game for a little while longer. At least until she figured out how to get away.

"How long have you lived here?" she asked, steering him from thoughts of Audrey or whatever the hell he thought he'd do with her while her child was gone.

He gave a little shrug and let the gun dangle at his side. "A few months. Being away from you and Audrey was torture. Moving here made me feel so much closer to you both. Plus I was able to get everything ready. Just the way I knew you'd like it."

As much as she didn't want to continue this conversation, she needed another visual of the house. The blueprints she'd studied were detailed but seeing every inch of it herself would only aid her when it came time to escape. "I'd love to see what you've done with the place."

His smile grew. "Okay. The living room isn't very big, but it's plenty for the three of us. Don't you think?" He extended an arm to the room at her right, waiting for her to explore.

She advanced over the threshold, the soft carpet cushioning her steps. The beige walls were filled with framed photos of candid snapshots she'd never known were taken. Her pushing Audrey on the swing in their backyard, a picture of her sitting on a bench with the sunlight streaming on her face, a photo of her and Audrey eating ice cream and laughing. A picture of Audrey sleeping in her bed that raised the hairs on Elizabeth's neck.

Pressing a trembling hand to her stomach, she commanded her nerves to settle so he wouldn't hear the quiver threatening to shake her vocal cords. "This is lovely, and plenty big enough. And the kitchen is connected which makes it all bright and airy." She noted the two doors in the kitchen. One, she knew, led to the attached garage. The other to the deck.

"There are two bedrooms and one bath. Audrey loved that I made hers identical to the one at your place. I'm so glad I made that key so I could come and go whenever I needed. It really helped get all the details right—to make sure I didn't miss anything when putting this place together." He chuckled. "She's a funny kid. You've done so well as a single mother, and now, she'll have a daddy too."

Tears prickled the corners of Elizabeth's eyes, but this time, rage formed them. How dare this man ever believe he could be Audrey's father? Claim that right through sheer force and manipulation?

But she couldn't let him see her change of mood, her anger. She entered the kitchen, running a finger along the smooth granite on the counter. A wooden knife block near the stove caught her attention. A knife was no match against a gun, but she'd feel more secure if she had a weapon. The only question was how Sebastian would react if she went after one.

She opted to take a step closer to the stove but kept her attention on the gray-tinted cabinets. "This looks like the same stain I have in my house."

Sebastian let out a long breath. "I'm glad you noticed. It was a bitch getting the right shade. I want you to feel at home. To know this is your space as much as mine. We'll be so happy here."

She squeezed her eyes shut, not knowing how much more she could handle.

"What's wrong?"

The heat of his body singed her, and her eyes flew open. He was close—too close. His chest nearly brushing against hers. Her lower back pressed against the counter, and Sebastian trapped her in place with an arm on each side. Using her peripheral vision, she judged the distance to the knives. If she could get a little more room, she might be able to just reach the thick, black handle.

She swallowed hard, unsure of how to answer.

He narrowed his eyes, and a mixture of concern and irritation clouded his green irises. "You don't look happy. Don't you realize everything I've done to get us here—to this moment when we can finally be together?" He slapped his empty palm against the counter to accentuate his words.

She winced. Her mind raced. She tried to recall all her years of training and work, but it'd been so long since she was with the FBI and used those skills, and dammit, this was different and the turmoil boiling her gut couldn't be contained any longer.

Noting Sebastian's loosened grip on the gun which rested beside her on the counter, she decided it was time for a different approach. "Of course I'm not happy. I keep picturing you pointing a gun at my child. Did you think I'd just bounce back from that? Forget you threatened her?"

He blinked in rapid succession, as if confused by her outburst. "I thought you'd understand why I did that. I wouldn't have hurt her. I promise."

"Did you know her father was killed by a gun? Was shot while in the line of duty and never even got to meet her because of it? Then you used that same weapon—made me imagine her dying the same way." Tears rolled down her face, and she let them fall. Let him see the pain he'd caused her. If she was lucky, he'd feel attached enough that he'd want to comfort and not hurt her.

"Oh, geez. I didn't even think of that. I'm sorry." With his free hand still pressed against the edge of the counter, he lifted his other one and rubbed the back of his neck, leaving the gun on the counter.

Without wasting a second, she grabbed the gun and ducked under his arm. She aimed the weapon at his chest. "Put your hands up. Now."

Frowning, Sebastian clicked his tongue. "You're not going to shoot me. You're my soul mate."

She turned off the safety and hooked her finger over the trigger. "Hands up. Now," she repeated.

He took a step forward. "Come on, Lizzie. Don't be stupid. Put down the gun."

The use of the nickname only Tucker ever used, and the disparaging tone, were the last straw. She tightened her muscles and pulled the trigger.

Nothing happened.

Sebastian laughed. "You didn't really think I'd put bullets in there and risk shooting Audrey, did you? Now be a good girl and put down the gun."

Anger and fear collided inside her. Bullets or not, she wouldn't go down without a fight. With the gun raised in her fist, she lunged forward and slammed the heavy weapon against the side of his head.

He grabbed her arm and yanked it down as blood oozed from a gash at his temple.

She wailed out a scream and brought her knee up to his groin. She wouldn't—couldn't—let him win.

He crumbled onto the floor and groaned.

Desperation spurred her forward. She had to get the hell out of here. He wouldn't stay down long. She darted for the French doors behind the four-person table. Her heart pounded as she fiddled with the handle a full two seconds before she realized it was locked. Unlocking it, she flung the door open. Fresh air hit her face and smelled like freedom.

A hard yank on her hair pulled her backward. Pain erupted as her skull screamed.

No!

She'd come too far, fought too hard. She thrashed around and tried to hit him with the gun she still held.

He circled her wrist with his firm grip and bent her arm until she dropped the weapon. "You won't leave me like the rest of them. Not now. Not ever."

She struggled against his hold, but he spun her around and backhanded her across the face. Her mouth throbbed and the tinny taste of blood flooded her senses.

He pulled back his fist, hatred twisting the lines of his face.

She braced for the blow and planned her next move. Fury sparked to life inside her. This man had put her through hell, but she wouldn't give up.

A fierce growl broke through her concentration. A streak of black fur barged inside the kitchen and flew toward Sebastian.

"What the hell?" Sebastian released her and held up his hands to shield himself from the furious canine.

Otto chomped down on his arm and tackled him to the ground. Menacing snarls mingled with Sebastian's cries for help.

Tucker and Cruz ran inside with guns drawn.

"Otto, heel," Tucker said as he gathered Elizabeth in his arms.

Cruz slapped handcuffs on a whimpering Sebastian and hauled him to his feet as he announced Sebastian's rights and ushered him outside.

Relief rushed over her like a tidal wave, and she collapsed against Tucker. Tremors shook her body and she held on tight. "Audrey? Where's Audrey?"

Tucker framed her face with his hands and pressed kisses to her cheeks, her chin, her mouth. "She's safe. Everyone's safe. Are you hurt? Did he touch you?"

She shook her head, hardly able to process how quickly the situation had changed. "I'm fine. I need to see Audrey."

He frowned and wiped something from the corner of her mouth. "You're bleeding."

She gingerly touched her lips and winced. "He hit me. He was so mad. He would have punched me, but Otto saved me. Oh, Otto!" Dropping to her knees, she threw her arms around the dog's neck.

Otto licked her face.

She laughed, and Tucker dropped down beside them. "He's the best boy there is."

"Mommy!"

The sound of Audrey's voice made Elizabeth's heart leap. She turned as Lincoln walked Audrey inside and she flung herself forward, one arm around Elizabeth and the other around Otto.

"Baby girl, are you okay?"

"I'm fine, Mommy."

Elizabeth wasn't sure about that, the trauma of what Audrey had experienced would stay with her for years to come, but she was safe and for now that's all that mattered.

Tucker wrapped them in a giant hug. "We're all fine," he said. "And I'll make sure we stay that way."

She connected her gaze with his and grinned. Fate had delivered her another blow, but she'd found Tucker again because of it. And now, together, they'd move on from this tragedy. Stronger and with new hope for a brighter future.

THE LAST DRIPS of sunlight bled into the darkening sky. Elizabeth sipped her wine and watched dusk sweep in and transform the world around her, taking away the lingering remnants of dread. Like Audrey, the trauma of today would stay with her, but for tonight, she just wanted to relish the simplicity of the evening.

Tucker stepped onto the deck and took a seat beside her on the swing. He wrapped one arm around her shoulders. "Audrey's all tucked in with her ever-present watchdog by her side."

"Thank you." She studied his handsome face and marveled at how she'd been lucky enough to find such a wonderful man twice in her life. The first time with Gary—a man who'd shown her what true love was and given her the best gift in the entire world in their daughter. And now with Tucker—a man who stepped in and loved her and her child like he was always meant to.

Her mouth went dry. Love. No doubt lingered in her mind where her feelings lay. She loved Tucker, and if she'd learned nothing else, it was life was unpredictable. Holding back wasn't something she wanted to do. Not anymore.

"What's that look for?" he asked, the side of his mouth hitched up.

"There you go again. Reading me like a book." Steeling her nerves, she set down her wine and hiked one knee up on the swing so she could face him better. "I can't begin to tell you how grateful I am for everything you've done for me and Audrey. I don't even want to know what the outcome of this whole terrifying situation would have been without you."

"There's nowhere in this world I would have rather been. But I've got to be honest, I've never been more scared in my life. When Sebastian pointed that gun at Audrey, then you ran into the house. I was so torn. I couldn't lose either of you."

"I knew you'd find a way to get to me," she said. "And I knew you'd take care of her if anything happened. I trust you with my everything."

"I trust you too, just try not to run into the home of an obsessed sociopath again and we should be fine."

She couldn't help but laugh. "Now that Sebastian's in jail, I don't think we'll have to worry about that happening."

After Tucker whisked her and Audrey away from the hellhole that Sebastian called home, Cruz had been in constant contact. Letting them know when Sebastian had been booked and giving them what details he could concerning Sebastian's confession.

A small part of her pitied him. She understood how deep

losing a loved one could cut, how all-consuming grief could be, but that didn't excuse his actions. Losing his fiancée a couple years prior didn't give him an excuse to terrorize others. No matter how delicate his mental state.

Tucker captured her hands. "The only thing I'm worried about is how much I'm going to miss you and Audrey when you leave."

"We'll be around as often as you want." She sucked in a shaky breath. "We love being here with you."

"You love it here, huh?" He grinned and wiggled his eyebrows.

Oh, boy. Here we go.

"We love *you*. *I* love you."

All amusement fled his face.

Her pulse thundered in her ears. Anxiety tightened the muscles in the pit of her stomach. Nothing mattered outside this moment, and Tucker's reaction. She hoped it wasn't too much too soon and wouldn't scared him off.

"Lizzie, I've wanted to hear these words from you for so damn long. I've loved you since the first time I saw you, and our time together the last few days has only strengthened that love. Strengthened our bond."

Her heart soared and she circled her arms around his neck and kissed him hard.

The sound of a tiny giggle forced her away from Tucker. Audrey stood in the doorway and covered her mouth with her hand as she laughed. "If you love Mommy and Mommy loves you, does that mean we get to stay here forever?"

"Honey, I would love nothing more," Tucker said, grinning.

"Yay!" Audrey jumped onto Tucker's lap.

Otto barked and jumped on Elizabeth with his front paws.

"Do you really mean it?" she asked. "You want us to stay with you?"

"He already said yes, Mommy."

"Yeah," Tucker said on a laugh. "What Audrey said."

Happiness exploded inside her, and she engulfed the ones she loved the most in her arms and held them tight. Life was a precious gift, and she couldn't wait to start this new journey with Tucker by her side, the partner she'd always wanted. The family she'd always dreamed of.

EPILOGUE

The crisp autumn breeze rustled around the ever-changing leaves. Tucker breathed in the fresh, mountain air, grateful as hell for the life he led. His dogs ran around the penned in yard beside the kennel, excited to chase the bright yellow balls Audrey whipped around. The girl might have a future as a pitcher, if that's what she wanted.

But so far, Audrey was delighted to run and play with the dogs and traipse around the retreat gaining adoring fans. In the last five months, every staff member at Crossroads Mountain Retreat had fallen in love with her. Something he'd done at very first sight, and that love had only grown since.

"Tucker, can you tell me another story about my daddy?" Audrey asked, sidling up beside him.

"Sure. Let's see. Have I told you about the time your daddy fell in the lake when we went fishing?"

Giggling, she shook her head. "That sounds silly."

"Your daddy was the silliest." He launched into the story he hadn't thought of in years and another piece of him healed— another part of his soul was reborn. Having Audrey in his life had brought him more joy than he'd ever imagined possible. With Audrey to fill his days and Elizabeth to fill his nights, he couldn't be happier.

Audrey bounced on her toes and gasped. "Wait. Mommy's coming!"

"Okay. It's showtime little one. You ready?"

She gave one heart-felt nod. "Ready."

He hurried to grab what he needed while Audrey waited with the dogs. When he came outside, Elizabeth unhooked the gate and gave a little wave.

"Otto should be tired after that hike. I know I am."

He still couldn't believe how bonded Elizabeth had become to Otto, but he would be forever grateful. "Thanks for taking him. He was getting a little restless."

"Was Audrey good?" she asked.

"Always, but I promised her a walk by the lake. Wanna join?" He held out a hand and waited for her to take hold.

"Sure. Audrey? You ready?"

Audrey skipped over and led the way to the walking path that wound around the lake. She held something in her hand, but kept it pressed to her chest as she charged ahead.

"What does she have?" Elizabeth asked.

"You'll see." He steered along to a spot where the mountains loomed tall in the distance and the sound of waves lapping onto the pebbled shore mingled with the singing birds over-head. "Before she shows you, I want to tell you how much I love you. How much I love Audrey and the life we've started to build together."

Confusion knitted Elizabeth's brow, suspicion clear on the turning of her lips. "I love our life, too."

"Good. Audrey. You're up."

He took a step backward and allowed space for Audrey to squeeze between them, Otto forever at her side. She handed over the gift the two of them had picked out for Elizabeth. "This is for you, Mommy."

Elizabeth pressed fingers to her mouth. She traced the photo in the frame with the pad of her thumb. "How did you get this?"

"Well, I wanted to give you something to show you how much I respect the life you had before. The life Gary gave you and I know is sad as hell he missed out on. A woman here teaches art classes, and I gave her a picture of Gary and asked her to make something special. So she painted this picture of the two of them together."

Tears welled in Elizabeth's eyes. "Audrey's on his lap. His baby girl. Sitting with him and smiling. I never thought I'd have a picture of the two of them together. Thank you."

"It's me and my daddy," Audrey said, her chest puffed with pride. "We kinda look alike."

Elizabeth laughed. "A little bit, honey."

"I love you so much, Lizzie." Tucker dropped to one knee and lifted a black velvet box. "I promise you that your past will always have a place in our present. But I want to be your future. Yours and Audrey's. If you'll have me."

"I'll have you every damn day for the rest of our lives, Tucker."

Joy expanded his chest. He opened the box, which revealed two rings. One with a diamond solitaire nestled between two ruby stones, the other with a tiny pearl on a gold band. He slid the diamond on Elizabeth's finger then stood and crushed his mouth to hers before he plucked the second ring from the cushion. "And this one's for you," he said, kneeling in front of Audrey.

Audrey widened her hazel eyes. "Me?"

He grabbed her tiny hand and put the ring on her finger. "Audrey. I promise to love you every day. I promise to tell you lots of silly stories about your daddy and make new memories with you. I promise to take care of you and teach you everything I know."

She launched herself into his arms. "I know I already have a daddy, but can I call you daddy, too?"

He glanced up at Lizzie, not knowing what to say. How to respond.

With tears streaming, she beamed.

That was all the approval he needed. He sniffed back tears, his heart beyond full. "Sweetheart, I'd be honored if you called me Daddy."

Sweeping her onto his hip, he squeezed her tight then looped an arm around the small of Elizabeth's back and pulled her close. He'd never understand how he got so lucky to end up in such a beautiful place with two beautiful ladies he loved with his whole being.

And a life that couldn't possibly get any better.

～

NEW to the Injured Heroes Series? Find out how it all begin in Crossroads of Revenge

DON'T MISS out on Grace and Zeke's fast-paced, second chance love story in Crossroads of Betrayal

ACKNOWLEDGMENTS

As always, a huge shout out to my husband and children who supported and encouraged me while writing this book. You will never understand how much your to-do lists and fun notes mean to me and keep me motivated. Fun fact, these notes and lists are from my kiddos and are dotted around my office!

Thanks to everyone who helped shaped this book. To Samantha Wilde, I'll forever be grateful our paths crossed. Between being an amazing critique partner and an amazing friend, I'll never know how I got so lucky. And to Julie Anne Lindsey, I always joke that you're the hardest editor I've ever had! Your notes and guidance have aided in my growth as a writer and a person and I'm so thankful for you.

A special thanks to April Bennett, aka The Editing Soprano, my incredible editor. This is our first book together and definitely won't be our last! You made my words shine! And as always, thank you to Deranged Doctors for such a beautiful cover!

Last but certainly not least, thank you to my readers! I am honored you'd spend your precious time picking up my book and giving me a chance. You are the best!
Danielle M Haas

ABOUT THE AUTHOR

Danielle M Haas is a stay-at-home mom turned author. When she isn't writing fast-paced romantic suspense novels with mysteries to live for and romance to die for, she's busy being a taxi driver to her two busy kids and forcing her introverted self to talk to other soccer moms. Her kids and husband are her world, which is also shared with her hyper Bernie doodle, two sassy cats, and one leopard gecko who's happy to chill on a rock all day. Her days are packed with cuddles, kisses, and a brain constantly thinking of new ways to create danger and romance for her next book.

ALSO BY DANIELLE HAAS

Injured Pride Series

Crossroads of Revival - Prequel Novella

Crossroads of Revenge

Crossroads of Delusion

Crossroads of Redemption

Murders of Convenience Series

Matched with Murder

Booked to Kill

Driven to Kill

The Sheffield's Series

Second Time Around

A Place In This World

Coming Home

Stand Alones

Bound by Danger

Girl Long Gone